The ACJ
-Advent, Christmas
Epiphany-

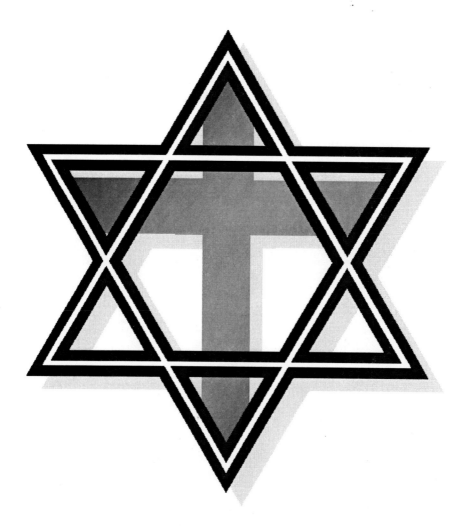

Richard Paul Dickinson

© 2005 by RPDickinson All rights reserved

Contents

	Pages
Contents:	2
Forward:	3-8
Introduction to the ACE seasons:	9-20

Daily readings:
-For the Season of Advent:

-Week 1 - The Hope of the coming Messiah, Jesus	21-48
-Week 2 - The Prophecy of the coming Messiah, Jesus	49-70
-Week 3 - The Forerunner of the coming Messiah, Jesus	71-89
-Week 4 - The Annunciation of the coming Messiah, Jesus	9-105
-Christmas Eve	106-107
-Christmas Day	108-111
-For the Season of Christmas (inc. Christmas Day)	108-139
-For the start of the Season of Epiphany	140-143
-Epiphany	140-143

Ending:	144
Appendices:	145-153
1. Brief comparison of Advent and Lent	145-146
2. Glossary	147-148
3. Alphabetical list of Advent, Christmas & Epiphany Activities	149
4. Advent, Christmas & Epiphany planner / calendar	150
5. Your own notes	151
6. Days of Advent Table	152
7. Miscellaneous resources	153

Forward

This book examines the seasons of Advent, Christmas and the start of Epiphany. It originally arose from a wish to use Advent to best advantage, to explore, study and learn about it and be able to relate and interact with it fully. Advent is then followed by the seasons of Christmas and Epiphany, and as these are all closely associated with one another, these are also considered and included in this book (though only the start of the celebration of Epiphany is included). The definition of Advent means "coming" (from Latin), and refers to the Christian Church's season coming before the birth of Jesus Christ, at Christmas. As such, Advent is concerned primarily with the events immediately before the birth of Jesus, who Christians believe to be the Son of God, promised Messiah and Saviour of man. Christmas Day is the holy day of celebration commemorating Jesus' birth (see the Glossary appendix for all other definitions) and is the start of the season of Christmas. The season of Christmas continues in all for a period of twelve days, being concerned with the immediate events after the birth and celebrating these. Then the season of the Epiphany begins which mainly marks the revelation of Jesus to the whole world, as represented by the involvement of the Wise Men.

Belief in God, Jesus and the Holy Spirit is an issue of faith. While non Christians do not have this belief and faith in Jesus, the life and death of Jesus Christ has had more impact on the world than the life and death of any other person in history. The Advent events that are described in the Bible show the interaction and relationship between God and man, at and during this time. Exploring the Advent, Christmas and Epiphany seasons can help our knowledge and understanding of God and man. Christians believe in one God who created everything in existence, notably including the universe, the world and all life especially mankind. Most Christians believe that the whole character of God can never be fully understood by man's reasoning alone, but that knowledge of and belief in God is necessary for a completely fulfilling life. These seasons and the events they relate to consequently have much importance for all mankind, and especially for Christians.

Many Christians also believe that God has a unique and special, tripart (or Trinitarian) state. That is, God is one entity, with three forms, those of God the Father, God the Son and God the Holy Spirit. While seeming masculine in character, God is beyond gender. God is often called God the Father, though could more completely be given the name, God, the Father and Mother. God exists in a different, (described as heavenly) spiritual dimension, and cares for all His creation, especially for mankind. Christians proclaim that God is goodness, but unfortunately there is a spirit force opposed to God, called either the Devil or Satan, representing the opposite of goodness i.e. evil and sin. The Devil helped corrupt God's creation by corrupting man. This was through Adam and Eve, the first man and woman made by God at the start of creation, and who the Devil encouraged to sin against God. By this sin of Adam and Eve, engineered by the Devil, the special pure relation between God and man was destroyed. It has since then always remained true that for man to wilfully behave badly is a sin before God. Thankfully however, God has power over everything, including sin and the Devil. God took compassion on man and promised to restore the relationship between Him and man, and this was to be achieved through a Messiah (which means anointed by God, to be the deliverer or saviour of mankind). Christians believe this Messiah to be Jesus, Son of God, man's saviour.

Advent then refers to the coming of Jesus, the Messiah, sent by God, and which we can relate to in the past, the present or the future. The Messiah Jesus (these names mean anointed saviour), as the first, and only, born Son of God is male, in the same way Adam, the first made human from God was male. As a male Jew, Jesus was circumcised, and experienced a fully human life, yet remaining fully divine. Jesus lived as a single unmarried man, as marriage to a woman would serve no purpose, either in the role and also nature of Jesus (i.e. as Messiah, and Son of God). Jesus though valued the state of marriage and the commitment a husband and wife make to one another and to all of their family, through marriage. While Jesus never married, many think of Jesus as being wedded to the Church of God. This is the Christian Church that Jesus called His followers to establish and all people to belong to. As Son of God, Jesus called all people His family, and encouraged all, especially Christians, to do likewise. God loves and created men and women equally, and He loves all His creation. God's love is purer than we can imagine, not an impure love, as one of power or sex or wealth is. Simply a love for His work of the goodness of creation. The nearest we can get to describing it in human terms is that of fatherly and motherly, or parental, love. It is though, a limitless love for mankind, which is amazing to contemplate and certainly beyond mankind's own personal experience of love. So while God's love may be described as fatherly, motherly or brotherly or sisterly at times, while this may be a good human analogy, in reality God's love always goes beyond human experience. Importantly, God, and so also God's love are good, and knowledge and experience of these facts can lead to completely fulfilled human lives.

Bearing this in mind we return to Advent, that is the season before the coming of God in the world as His Son, through the incarnation (being made human) and birth of Jesus Christ, Son of God. Jesus came as Messiah and Saviour, to lead all people to God and to free mankind from sin, allowing man to be with God eternally. These roles will be seen through the Advent and Christmas Bible readings in this book. A Christian is anyone who believes Jesus to be the Son of God, and as Jesus has said, by default this also means believing in God the Father and God the Holy Spirit. The start of Advent marks the start of the Church's New Year. It is the start of the part of the Christian story that tells of the events immediately prior to the birth of Jesus. The rest of the Christian story then continues up to the present day and then will continue on eternally. The complete Christian story is the complete story of Jesus Christ, Son of God, Messiah and Saviour of mankind. This whole Christian story includes this Advent period, and continues with the life and ministry of Jesus, and then also the death, resurrection and ascension of Jesus. It continues further with the establishment of the Christian Church, right up to this present time, and as just stated, will carry on forever (eternally).

However, returning to Advent, it is not simply a waiting period before Christmas. In fact, as well as now being aware that Christmas is coming soon, it is the time to prepare and get ready for this coming birth of Jesus the Messiah. We need to be prepared and ready spiritually as well as physically, and Advent is the right time to do this. In the Anglican (Church of England) Church structure, the Advent season is roughly four weeks long. It is divided into four weekly parts, each with a separate theme, beginning with Advent Sunday, which is the fourth Sunday before Christmas Day. Advent finishes on Christmas Day, on the twenty fifth of December. This means Advent varies in length, depending on whether Advent Sunday is early (earliest is Nov. 27th) or late (latest Dec. 3rd). There are sufficient readings in this book to start with Advent Sunday on November 27th and go through to Christmas Eve. For the years when Advent Sunday is later, the last few days of Advent week four can be omitted, to move to Christmas Eve at the appropriate point. (See table, Days of Advent, at Appendix 6). It can be helpful to look at the calendar now, and to decide which days readings will be used in Advent week four, that correspond to the calendar days of this current year. Many Christian Churches (Roman Catholic, Anglican and others) follow this general pattern and so also does this book.

In the first week of Advent, the Church focuses on the hope and belief of the coming of God in the form of His Son, the promised Messiah and the daily readings here examine this. In the second week, the readings look at the prophecies concerning the Messiah. In the third week, we start to look at the events immediately prior to Jesus' birth. Especially we study the role of John the Baptist who proclaimed and pointed to the prominence of Jesus. John was a special person chosen by God, born by a miracle almost at the same time as Jesus, and who later was the catalyst to start Jesus' ministry. Then, in the readings for the fourth week of Advent, we can look closely at the way God revealed His plan of Jesus' birth, and all the details (people and events), involved with this, and culminating with the birth, of Jesus at Christmas. From then, we continue with appropriate readings in the season of Christmas, for twelve days, and come to the start of Epiphany, which is the end of this book.

So, to start with, we follow these Advent themes building up to the coming birth of Jesus. It is both helpful and interesting to know what the events were that led up to and shaped the birth of Jesus, as the role and life of Jesus is crucial to the existence of Christians and the Church alike. These themes are as a framework to help us know, appreciate and understand this coming event, and the factors leading up to it, all contained within the Advent season. However, we do not have to be limited or bound by this themed structure and can think of and use any other ideas that may be useful to further help us through this time. Bearing this in mind, this book can act as a guide to, and through Advent Christmas and the start of Epiphany. As stated, it is based on a daily structure of Bible readings, which are relevant to the Advent, Christmas and Epiphany events and themes. At the end of each daily Bible reading and discussion from that, there is a further Bible reference given along with headings for prayer, action and notes. A short prayer has been included for each day, but it is good to use this as a reminder to think of a prayer of your own. Also, the action and notes headings are reminders for your own use.

Life can be seen as a daily journey, which takes us along different paths and experiences, and the Christian life is special because Christians acknowledge on our daily journey we are with God, Jesus and the Holy Spirit. The Advent, Christmas and Epiphany seasons, as a part of life's experience, can also be seen and experienced as a daily journey with God. In today's busy world there are many activities demanding our attention and action and often and especially during this Advent season, many more activities can occur. We need to try to ensure that we also have time to attend to our spiritual activities (often in association with prayer and worship), to have a good relationship with God, during these seasons. We can experience a relation with

God through many appropriate activities, but need a balance of spiritual activity also. Prayer is one important example of an activity that can involve spiritual action and reaction (remember though, prayer dialogue involves listening and conversing). Jesus himself stressed the role of prayer and spiritual activity, and highlighted man's need for the holiness of God, leading to both physical and spiritual wellbeing. So attending to appropriate physical and spiritual exercises and activities will help us, and others, to live our lives as God intended, under His care. We can do this individually and collectively, and it is important we get our priorities right at this time, and focus on God and not religious rote or other distracting observances and practices.

In the UK today, it is reported that many people, both children and adults, do not know the Advent and Christmas Christian stories. Most people notice changes at this time, though many are unaware of the real reason for the season. Many wrong reasons are quoted e.g. Santa Claus, charity, national and family celebrations time. Often the birth of Jesus and the knowledge that He is the Son of God is not known, or is ignored. This Advent story is interesting and exciting and has much that is relevant to life and it has inspired countless numbers of people, with the birth of Jesus being the climax of Advent. It contains many potential controversies, which is not surprising as it comes from the Bible, possibly the most influential and controversial book known to man. As we read about Advent, Christmas and Epiphany through this book, then we can relate our understanding of these seasons to our own circumstances, and experiences.

Advent, being the Church's New Year, is the first season in the Church's own yearly calendar. This calendar allows us to follow biblical events of importance in a logical, ordered progression. As we follow this structure we can learn about these important events and explore them as fully as we wish to. This will help build, reinforce and therefore, strengthen our own personal faith. We should then share our knowledge and understanding and beliefs of Advent with others, both in and out of the Church. This will help build our corporate, communal faith. Just as each year has natural seasons, so the Church's yearly calendar follows Christian seasons (other seasons include Lent, Easter, and Trinity). This calendar is somewhat arbitrary and imprecise but has value in providing a general framework, and the precise timings of events while of some interest, are not essential to be fixed or agreed on. It is good enough that this general calendar is agreed on by the Christian Church (albeit with minor differences i.e. western orthodox Christianity compared to eastern orthodox Christianity date differences). In the western orthodox church, the date of Christmas Day for example was set by the Roman Catholic church as 25 December. It is possible that Jesus was born before this, maybe in the previous September. It could be instead, that Jesus was conceived around the 25 December, but these details, while of some interest and importance, again are not essential for an understanding of and response to the Advent, Christmas and Epiphany events. Record keeping and knowledge of chronology was not as precise at the time Jesus lived compared to today. If you wish to investigate these matters further then you need to do more study, which is beyond the scope of this book. Such information can be found elsewhere (in other books and on Internet sites, some of which are mentioned in the appendix).

As each year passes though, we need to be able to look afresh at the important events that occur during these seasons. We should not take any of these seasons and events for granted but we need to cherish each and every one anew and see it in new light, as renewal should be. So, mindful of this, take a fresh look at Advent, Christmas and Epiphany this year, and every year.

Finally, it is often said, that God is love and as Christians, we can see God's love at this time in the Advent Christmas & Epiphany stories and seasons. Christians should show all people their love of God, or expressed another way; Christians should reflect God's love at this time to all people (and especially those in need). In the Old Testament the emphasis is on man's love to and between friends. While with Jesus' arrival, the New Testament is born and the emphasis is on the need for man's love towards all people, also and especially, our enemies or even just those we like less than we should. In fact as Jesus said, we should love ourselves and all others in the same way that God loves us. Thus, this signals the beginning of a new relationship with God and with ourselves.

Introduction to the ACE seasons

Now we know Advent is the time relating to the coming of the birth of Jesus, and importantly that it is not just a period of waiting for Jesus' birth. So the Advent season starts with the announcement of the coming of the birth of Jesus, the hoped for Messiah, and continues with the preparation for this birth. We are told of Jesus' birth in two of the four Gospels (Matthew and Luke - Mark and John omit these details and concern themselves mainly with Jesus' ministry). These accounts are from the first books in the New Testament section of the Bible. It is generally, but by no means universally, accepted that Jesus' birth was a real historical event, and Christians accept this, in just the same way as we accept that we were born into the world. So we Christians know that Jesus was a real person, but who lived over two thousand years ago. As well as the Gospels we have the records of Josephus an early Jewish historian, Tacitus the early Roman historian and Pliny the younger, Roman governor of Turkey. What is so much harder to know is that Jesus was and is God's Son. Christians believe this absolutely, even though the Annunciation and Virgin birth may be difficult conceptually to comprehend. There is a similar difficulty of comprehension of God coming to exist on earth as man by way of His Son and leaving His Spirit with us after Jesus' Ascension (His departure from earth, after His resurrection, to heaven).

Not everything in the Bible should be taken literally, as for example in many places the parables and descriptions from Jesus show Him using metaphorical illustrations. However, many events and miracles in the Bible in my opinion could be, and I believe, were done by a God who made the whole of creation. The exact detail of these cannot be comprehended by man without knowledge from God, and while it is interesting to speculate on all these events, without being given this complete knowledge and explanation from God, man will never comprehend these fully. The Christian position is clear, man can believe only in man and not in God, and so will miss out on a totally fulfilling and eternal life. Or, man can believe in the wholeness of God, Jesus and the Holy Spirit, and so experience a fulfilling and eternal life. The Advent story is a remarkable one, as is the full story of Jesus' life on earth and return to heaven, which is told in all the Gospels, in the New Testament part of the Bible. The Bible records the important witness of God's Word and workings through man, from the start of the world (God's creation), to about two thousand years ago, with the coming of the Messiah and start of the new Christian Church. It has two sections, the Old and the New Testaments. The Old Testament can be seen as the prelude to the New Testament. So, in many ways the Old Testament is the advent to the coming of Jesus and His ministry, which is recorded in the New Testament. We can look at the Old Testament and see the references to the coming of the Messiah and we can see how these references are substantiated and validated by Jesus and His actions, confirming to Christians that He is the Son of God. Jesus Himself is unique; as at the same time as being the Son of God, He is also the Son of Man. Jesus is fully divine and also fully human at the same time. Just as God is a unique entity, so is Jesus, and so also is the Holy Spirit. Coincidentally or not, every human that God has created is unique in some way too. It appears that in God's human creation exact clones were not wanted (each human made in the image of God, and unique).

In the Old Testament the books of the prophets and leaders of the Israelite nation point to the coming of the Messiah who is to be the saviour for God's chosen people, the Jews. In the New Testament the books of the apostles and first Christians show the Messiah to have come to all people (Jews and Gentiles alike) through and in the person of God's Son Jesus Christ. To know and comprehend Advent we need to read the Bible, both the Old and New Testaments. Advent is the Church's time of year when we concentrate more on those parts of the Bible that point to and show us the build up and preparation for the coming birth of Jesus. This is a very special time. Man had been promised a Messiah (saviour) by God and had been waiting for this Messiah to come for years. Some people had claimed to be the promised Messiah, but all were found wanting and false. Christians declare that Jesus however is the real deal, the one true Messiah and Saviour promised by, and sent by God. Everything about Jesus is special, and certainly the start of Jesus' life, coming to and being born on earth is part of that specialness.

If we wish to, we can think of Advent as being that very first Advent (which is how the Church chooses to have it described) with Joseph and Mary preparing to be parents to Jesus. We learn of and recall all the events leading up to Jesus' birth and circumstances of that. Firstly we have the story of the announcement of the miracle of the announced pregnancy and birth to come, for Elizabeth, Mary's cousin, told to her by the angel Gabriel. Elizabeth was old and had been thought to be physically unable to have children, but God gave her the ability to conceive. The angel Gabriel is an archangel, one of the leaders of the group of God's heavenly created beings, called angels (meaning Messenger). Then, about 6 months later, the angel Gabriel visited Mary and announced that Mary (an unmarried virgin) was also soon to have a child. This would be an even greater miracle. Again it was not to occur by normal human means, but in a unique way, by special intervention of God, and the baby would not be a normal human baby, but was to be the Son of God, and Messiah. This special baby though would be born in the normal way all human babies are born. The angel then told Joseph (who was already engaged to Mary) not to be worried by this situation, but to marry and support Mary. Both Mary and Joseph were obedient to these instructions and they married each other as they were originally planning, and undertook to be the earthly parents to the heavenly baby given by God. Soon after this Mary then visited her cousin Elizabeth, prior to the birth of Elizabeth's son, who was to be John the Baptist.

Just before the birth of John, Mary returned home to Nazareth and next we can think of the preparations that Mary and Joseph had to make as they waited for Jesus' birth. This is the birth of God's Son brought into the world by their efforts as the chosen ones by God for this purpose. Close to the time of the birth of Jesus, Mary and Joseph were obliged by Roman authority and order, to journey from their home in Nazareth, Galilee, and go to Bethlehem in Judea. There they had to be registered in the census being held to identify people's heritage (and thought to be related to tax purposes). When they arrived in Bethlehem the town was crowded, because of people coming to register in the census. One account of the story (Luke 2 v7) says there was no room at the inn for them. They couldn't find a suitable room anywhere to stay and they had to take shelter in stables with the animals, as Mary was ready and preparing to give birth. Another interpretation and possibility was that they went to a house and the upper room, which was the usual living and sleeping place was crowded, but that there was space on the ground floor, where often animals were kept inside houses. Here, an animal feeding trough or manger proved to be a suitable cot for the newly born baby Jesus. Whatever the exact detail, this was an emergency measure and made an unusual maternity and nursing ward, but they would have been grateful for even that (being better than giving birth in the open and so not having any privacy or security). Meanwhile angels came and announced the birth to the local shepherds, who then went to find and pay their respects to this special baby Jesus. This location (whether stable or animal area of a house) possibly made it easier for the shepherds to find and visit.

All the characters in the story have some significance, individually and collectively. Of course the angels bear testament to the supernatural side of this event. The shepherds signify the commoner human side, although God and Jesus used the example of a good shepherd often to describe how They also would lead Their followers (the sheep). There are other sheep comparisons. David, an honoured servant of God and later famous king of Israel, had been a shepherd. Also, sheep and lambs were used for sacrifices to God through the Old Testament. God had even asked Abraham to sacrifice his own son Isaac, for His sake, but then as Abraham was obedient, God substituted a ram. Jesus is often talked of as the Lamb of God. He was the perfect man and became the perfect sacrificial offering for the sin of mankind. Also He is called the Good Shepherd, with mankind described as the sheep. We can only ponder on this way chosen by God for Jesus to be born in the world. God chose a humble and difficult way but this set the tone that Jesus His Son came into the world to help all men and did not come into the world with God granting Him any special worldly favours.

We can consider the need for a Messiah to help man back to God, and we can see this became needed soon after man was created and disobeyed God (in the Garden of Eden). As a result, God disciplined both Adam and Eve, and the Devil. "And I will put enmity between you and the woman, and between your seed and her seed: He shall crush you on the head, and you shall bruise him on the heel", Genesis 3 v15. This passage shows us that the Devil (through the snake) had sought to corrupt God's creation, by turning man away from God. God puts this punishment of hatred between the Devil (the snake) and the woman, confirming that they will both hurt one another. This is confirmed through the Bible, with constant warfare between man and the Devil. The Devil seeks to corrupt all people including and especially the chosen people of God and is partly successful, but not wholly, as certain individuals remain faithful to God (Noah, Abraham and David notably). Nonetheless God promised to help man by sending a Messiah, but the Devil determined to stop this. In fact the Devil tried to prevent the birth of Jesus, shown by the action of wicked Queen Athaliah attempting to destroy the royal seed of the house of Judah (2 Chronicles 22 v10). Judah had been blessed by God (Gen. 49 v10) and a descendent from the line of Judah was expected to be the Messiah. God though preserves the royal lineage and seed in the infant Joash.

Now, in the Advent story we see the Devil has failed to prevent the birth of Jesus. Jesus is the Messiah, born human yet fully divine, born of Mary a descendant of Eve. So instead the Devil tries through Herod the Great to have baby Jesus killed, but failed, as we will read later. The Devil later even tried to corrupt Jesus himself directly. When this also failed the Devil again tried through others to kill Jesus (Luke 4 v28), and, again unsuccessfully. The Devil then tried to harm and destroy Jesus through the crucifixion. Jesus though remained faithful to God and triumphed over the Devil when He rose from the dead and later ascended to heaven. By this, Jesus has overcome all sin and has become the way for all people to come to God fully and eternally. The Devil cannot prevail over God. Now through Jesus' action, and man's belief in Jesus, the Devil cannot prevail over man.

So we now see Jesus' birth as a monumental historic event which was looked forward to and hoped for all those long years ago. In particular, the Jews hoped that a Messiah and Saviour for the earth would arise, to conquer oppression, misery and pain and suffering. In our Advent today let us feel and have the hope and longing to have the Messiah and Saviour with us. Today we know Jesus the Messiah was born over two thousand years ago and has set us free. Also we know the Bible says Jesus will come again to bring His kingdom to earth and we must hope for that too (though we cannot expect this in any preconceived way, as it will only be done in God's way). So we can think back to the first Advent which started Christianity and now look forward to the next coming of Jesus, which will happen some time surely in the future. Although at that time Jesus will not be coming as a human baby, He will come as the complete divine king. Christians have a calling to tell others about Jesus, and to hope that they too will believe in Jesus and so become Christians also. As we have not lived at the time of Jesus, we have not met Him physically and so have to take a leap of faith to believe in Him. However, even many people who met Jesus during His life on earth, had to take that leap of faith, and whether that was made any easier by being with Jesus at the time may not always have been certain. What is certain to me, and all Christians, is the value of finding that personal relationship with Jesus, which leads to God and eternal salvation. Finding and then believing in Jesus becomes a time of change and this is what Advent most certainly is. Miraculous events took place at Advent (angels, virgin birth, and guiding star) and so it is a time that should be a miraculous special time to change our lives now.

At that first Advent not that many people knew its significance, but today many more people know this story, as it is told and remembered by Christians and even non Christians. When we know the Advent story we are able to explore its significance, and to re-evaluate this each and every Advent we experience. Yet as I have already said, there are still many who do not know the Christian Advent story and that Christmas is the birth of Jesus, God's Son. So it is important, that during this time of Advent, people who do not know the story can find out about it and then they will better know the importance and true meaning of Christmas (and I hope this book will help to achieve this). While for those that do know this story, it is a time to explore it further, and for Christians, a time to thank God and share the story with others. In doing so, it is clear that the Advent story has many paradoxes, however the whole Christian story also has many paradoxes.

Comparisons can be made between that first Advent season and now. Try and imagine Advent taking place today. Mary and Joseph may have travelled by car, taxi, or bus, or train, but would not have walked all the way from Nazareth to Bethlehem, with or without a donkey. They would have booked a room by telephone or Internet or stayed with friends or relatives. They would have wanted to know where the local hospital with maternity ward was. When they arrived there late at night and found they were double booked and there was little space, they had to look elsewhere. Joseph may have tried to make calls on his mobile phone to find other accommodation. There was nothing available and as it was late they took the offer of camp beds in the partly completed barn conversion behind the guesthouse. Alongside this was another barn that was in use partly as a temporary stable for the owner's horse and goat on the small holding that was attached, which was also soon to be developed into more accommodation and facilities for the guesthouse. Nevertheless, the weary couple hoped for a good night's rest and to sort things out the next day, but to round the day off, Mary went into labour. Joseph might have phoned for an ambulance (but as the batteries were low, the ambulance call was unsuccessful) and the baby was born in the early hours of the morning to the relief and amazement of everyone there. It is just possible therefore to imagine a modern day Advent story, which would superficially seem very different to the original, but overall Jesus is needed the same today as during the period He was born in, around two thousand years ago. Jesus the Messiah's character and principles are constant and timeless. Also man and his emotions and reactions are essentially similar also, with many places in the world today still experiencing oppression and injustices. The world is different now though, as the Messiah has come and has offered salvation to all people, and if all the world acknowledged this, then oppression and injustice would cease. This is the Advent hope now, which will be completely fulfilled when Jesus the Messiah returns again, to rule the earth. This is the second Advent, that God has promised will come, and that we also await now.

Traditionally then, Advent is remembered from the time of God's announcement to Mary of her pregnancy up to the birth of Jesus. In a broader sense though, it also spans the time when God first promised to send a Messiah and Saviour from the prophecies in the Old Testament, to the birth of Jesus at Christmas. Through the Old Testament times, the Jews often became tired of waiting for the Messiah and often dishonoured God. The prophets were men of God, ordained to call the Jewish nation back to God and remind them of the promise of the coming of the Messiah. With both scenarios Advent may be likened to the period of pregnancy before birth (in the former this would have been about nine months long and in the latter around nine hundred years long). In a biological way, life, which is fragile, is developing and needs protecting and nurturing spiritually and physically during pregnancy. In humans, a family change in relations occurs. Naturally men and women are affected differently by pregnancy and birth. Both are affected psychologically, but women are more affected physically. As pregnancy progresses changes happen and preparations may be required (provision for care, including food, clothing, warmth, shelter, etc). Pregnancy and then birth binds families and people together. Birth is the end of the act of creation which the parents are privileged to have participated in and initiated. It does bind and bond families and people together through love, and it brings responsibilities.

Advent, as the first part of the Christian story, has affected Christian and world culture, and we shall examine this throughout this study. Also, over time people have debated which Christian event, Christmas or Easter has most importance. This is mainly an academic theoretical point, as both events are crucial to the Christian story, and each event needs the other event so, in my opinion they are of mutual importance. A similar exercise can be done comparing the periods of preparation for these two events i.e. Advent and Lent. Both these times are used to get closer to God prior to each important Christian event that these lead to, birth at Christmas, and death and resurrection at Easter. Lent is often simply thought of as a time to give up something in order to come to God. In a similar simplistic way, I believe Advent can in contrast, be thought of as a time to take up something in order to come to God. Take up anything, e.g. reading, painting, building, singing, praying, acting, dancing, gardening, cooking, cleaning, writing, and especially helping others, in praise of the coming birth of Jesus the Messiah. Both giving something up, and taking something up for God, encourage self-discipline and commitment to God and other people, and so are helpful to refocus our service to God directly and primarily, and then indirectly and secondarily to man.

Throughout Advent and at Christmas many traditions are observed and we will mention some of these here and later in the daily readings. Many different traditions exist in different countries of the world and it is interesting to know and understand the similarities and differences we have in UK compared to other countries. Many towns hold fairs and markets to sell produce and gifts for Advent and Christmas. Food and drink and fairground rides are also available for adults and children, and these become places to meet and socialise. In big towns, these attract lots of people, and contribute to the cities' economy and employment. In Germany, the Christmas Markets in the big towns are very popular and attract tourists, though they are very commercially orientated, but many people enjoy them nonetheless. The crowds, with the noise and activity and lights and warmth, bring an atmosphere to the dark nights. Possibly there may have been a similar atmosphere in Bethlehem over two thousand years ago, when Mary and Joseph arrived into that crowded town. We remember though they were probably tired and were not thinking of socialising. Instead they were probably thinking of how to cope with the imminent birth and the future, knowing the baby was not only sent by God, but was to be the Son of God.

On the European continent many countries celebrate St Nicolas' Day on December 6th, and gifts are exchanged on this day mainly for children. Christmas Day is celebrated solely as Jesus' birthday. St Nicolas was a Christian bishop (he lived in Myra, now present day Turkey) who gave presents to deprived children and some give him the title of Santa Claus and others Father Christmas. In contrast, Ethiopia, which was said to have had the first Christian church, (started by the Ethiopian Eunuch who Phillip converted - Acts 8 v 26-40) celebrates Christmas on Jan 7th (the orthodox, eastern, non-catholic tradition). Jews celebrate Hanukkah, the festival of light, around this time of year. This celebrates the Jews regaining control of the Temple in Jerusalem (from foreign Greek, Syrian occupation) and restoring the worship of God and so helping to maintain the Jewish nation, to which Jesus the Messiah was soon to be sent to by God. There are Christians in many different churches celebrating Advent and beyond, with many different Christian traditions throughout the world. It can be interesting to examine these different customs, which often have symbolic Christian origins. However thankfully the main Advent and Christmas (and Epiphany) stories have the same basic elements, so all Christians can unite in acknowledging these common points.

The importance of the birth of Jesus is shown in our chronology of history. Somewhile after His life and death, the western civilised world's year dating was changed and Jesus' birth date was made the central reference point of this. This was actually done by a monk (Dionysius Exiguus, AD 525). Times, (dates/years) before Jesus' birth are numbered BC, Before Christ. Years after His birth are known as AD, Anno Domini (In the year of the Lord Jesus). This forms an important reference point for most of the world. Dionysius thought Jesus was born on March 25 in the year 754 of the then Roman calendar (March 25 most likely refers to the Annunciation). Dionysius put Jesus' birth at December AD 1. We now know that his calculations were wrong and in fact Jesus was probably born around four or five BC, but no change has been made to rectify this in the calendar we now use. For interest, the modern Jewish calendar begins from the supposed date of the Creation in 3760 BC. Also the ancient Roman calendar was based on the date of the foundation of the city of Rome in 753 BC, while the Greek calendar was dated from the first Olympic games, which by our calendar now, took place in 776 BC.

At the end of Advent in the UK generally on Christmas Day, December 25th, Christians celebrate Jesus' birth. However many, both Christians and non Christians encourage the story of yet another Christmas figure called Santa Claus, or Father Christmas, and there are many traditions associated with this mythical character. He is often thought of as St Nicolas, the kind Christian bishop who the Church made a saint, and has a remembrance day on December 6th and as stated earlier is celebrated more in European countries, especially Holland and Germany. Confusingly, there is yet another Santa, who delivers presents to all children especially, who have been good, on Christmas Eve night, some are placed in stockings, others under Christmas trees. In this fiction story Santa lives near the North Pole (possibly in Lapland) and spends the year there preparing toys for the children with his elf helpers. On Christmas Eve he flies round the earth in a sleigh and hands out the toys ready to be opened on Christmas Day. Christians should not confuse Advent and Christmas with waiting for a secular Father Christmas or Santa Claus which may be what the non-Christian world awaits. The Christian Advent awaits Father God, but in the form of God the Son, as Jesus Christ. Santa Claus is now a tradition from another story (St Nicholas possibly). Replicas of Santa are evident in many places, and he has become very familiar in western culture, but he has no connection to Jesus and the Advent story, and is in fact an intruder in this Christian Advent story. Santa then has become an alternative Advent story for non-believers, and an extra tolerated (and sometimes mistakenly encouraged) figure for many Christians. In contrast to Santa Claus, Jesus' birth is a historical fact. Santa Claus gives gifts to children especially who have been good. God gives everyone the gift of Himself, as Jesus, which is the best present anyone can ever have. Much of this Santa Claus story is to try to give children mainly, a sense of magic and mystery, though this is exactly what the Advent and Christmas nativity story has. So the Advent season has a completely different meaning for non Christians. Is it coincidence that Santa is an anagram of Satan? Whether this is significant is not fully known, but Christians do know Satan will use many ways to lead man away from God, especially subtle methods. Everyone needs to be on their guard against the ploys of Satan, through the Advent Christmas and Epiphany seasons and always.

Many other traditions during this time are shared by Christians and non Christians. For example Christmas trees have many Christian and some secular significances. For Christians, as evergreen trees they represent the everlasting nature of God. The fir tree also has significance with St Boniface who was converting pagans to Christianity in Germany. One time some pagans were about to kill a boy under an oak tree and St Boniface intervened and chopped the oak down and the story says a fir tree sprang up in its place and became associated with Christ after that. Another tree tale is apparently one winter's night Martin Luther, again in Germany, saw stars shining in the night through the branches of a fir tree and this reminded him of God coming from heaven to earth, and led to trees being decorated with candles as representing the stars. For non Christians, the trees represent a part of nature and often are decorated with many artefacts and symbols. We have also noted the increase and amount of commercial activity that happens during Advent in the build up to Christmas. This can cause problems, for instance excess spending can lead to debt and later misery. Also this secular (non religious) emphasis at this time leads to a danger of not spending enough time attending to the spiritual preparation which is in fact essential to allow the complete enjoyment and experience of the Advent, Christmas and Epiphany seasons. This may be thought of as a ploy by Satan to distract from the meaning and birth of Jesus.

However some secular activities can create good effect, as the Christmas pop song," Do they know it's Christmas?/ Feed the World", from Band Aid (Bob Geldorf, Midge Ure 1984) did for charity for the Ethiopian famine relief (and later Live Aid, organised by Bob Geldorf). Many of these Advent and Christmas traditions will be briefly mentioned throughout this guide. It is though important to spend some time on spiritual preparation as well as on secular preparation, and it is hoped that this guide can be of some help in the spiritual area.

In the Northern Hemisphere Christmas roughly coincides with the shortest day of the year. This, the winter solstice, has always been an important day since early/prehistory and as such was a time of celebration (and still is for some). The Romans celebrated this time as the feast of Saturnalia, and it was somewhat coincidental that the early Church chose Christmas Day to be fixed around this time. Some customs that we may observe at Christmas originate from this time (such as the Yule log) and have no direct association with Jesus and the account of His birth in the Bible. Man has always been influenced by nature and the natural world around him. Often Man has sought to control nature for his own benefit, but has seen that this is difficult to do in some instances. Many cultures have felt there is a spiritual side to nature and this led to a belief in gods and, or spirits controlling nature and later controlling the affairs of man. These gods have been worshipped in an attempt and hope that it may benefit the person, clan and culture worshipping them. As Christians we believe in One God who has created our existence and everything else, and we believe that we are called to God, to worship and serve God. Living to honour God pleases God, and God gives us His full blessing for doing this. It is very important to know and to be clear and focused on the true Christian story of Advent and separate facts from fiction and the secular from the spiritual. As already just mentioned, there is no Santa Claus or Father Christmas figure in the Christian Advent story, although God can be thought of as the Father of Christmas.
Looking back to that first Advent, we can think of Mary and Joseph's reactions to God's Advent plan. They were faithful and obedient to God, and this can be an example to us, to follow in our lives. They trusted God and God rewarded them by experiencing Jesus in a special way. We cannot experience their unique relation with Jesus, but we can find our own unique experience of Jesus, if we have not already done so. If we are Christians already this Advent time is a time to prepare to reaccept Jesus in our lives and strengthen our relation with God, Jesus and the Holy Spirit. If not Christians, it is a time to study and think of the relevance of the birth of Jesus, to individuals and to the world. For both Christians and non Christians it can be a time of renewal and of rebirth with God and Jesus, and the Holy Spirit. Many non Christians do see beyond the tinsel and trappings and find Jesus at this time, and commit themselves to love Him and so receive the salvation of God, the eternal life Jesus brings to all who love and believe in Him.

There are also many traditions associated with Epiphany. As some people in some places and countries still celebrate this day (January 6) as Jesus' birthday they exchange gifts at this time (in representation of the presents the Wise Men brought). Other traditions are associated with the three kings (or Wise Men or Magi). One of these concerns the story of Befana. According to this story as the Wise Men came to the manger they met an old woman, Befana, cleaning her house. Apparently they invited her to come with them, but she said she had to finish cleaning first and that she would follow them later. The story has it that Befana never found the manger and then she wandered the earth looking for Jesus (this story of Befana is traditional in parts of Italy and Russia). In Spain (and Spanish speaking countries like Mexico) this day is El Dia de los Reyes (the day of the Kings). Traditional Epiphany food is a "king's crown". This is a cake decorated and shaped as a king's crown with a trinket (or bean) inside. The person getting the piece with the trinket is of course the king for the day.

In the Eastern Orthodox Church Epiphany is also important as a celebration of Jesus' baptism, while the Catholic Church celebrates Jesus' baptism on January 9.

Finally, use this book as a guide and framework to explore and enjoy the seasons of Advent, Christmas and Epiphany. It contains some facts and also many personal thoughts and views. Use it as your own personal springboard, both for your thoughts and actions, to enrich you at this time of year, and for change and growth in your life (past, present and future). It can be used for study and read at any time of year, but is especially designed for use from the start of the Advent season and onward through Christmas to Epiphany, for daily reading and action. May it help prepare you to meet Jesus at the end of this Advent season coming, and let it also help prepare you to meet Jesus at the end of the final Advent season yet to come. For all Christians look forward to Jesus Christ our Saviour and Messiah returning from heaven to earth again and should prepare for this new season to come.

Advent Week 1
Main theme: The Hope of the coming Messiah Jesus
ADVENT SUNDAY 1

<u>Isaiah 52 v7-9 (RSV)</u>. *How beautiful on the mountains are the feet of him who brings good tidings, who publishes peace, who brings good tidings of good, who publishes salvation, who says to Zion, "Your God reigns". Hark, your watchman lift up their voice together, they sing for joy; for eye to eye they see the return of the Lord to Zion.*

Isaiah was a great Jewish prophet, and this verse is from his book in the Old Testament of the Bible. Isaiah lived in Jerusalem in the eighth century before the birth of Jesus. Here he tells how watchmen see God's return to Jerusalem, which is a reference to (and prophecy of) Jesus, the Messiah, coming to Jerusalem, to God's holy city on earth. Isaiah encourages the Jews that God will return to them.

Now is the start of the Advent season and it is our Christian marvellous, wonderful hope that the Lord God is coming to us in the person of Jesus, the Messiah, the Son of God and Saviour of Mankind. This prophecy of Isaiah is a direct reference to Jesus's coming and Ministry. Now all people can focus on this fact, that Jesus is to come and He is the Lord and Saviour of Mankind, God's Son, sent to conquer our sin and lead us all back to God. He is our promised Saviour and Messiah from God. God is the supreme divine being and creator, that man should serve, in honour and recognition that everything (in heaven and earth) is dependent on and originates from God. Christians believe that God has a Son (Jesus our Messiah and Saviour) and also a Spirit, that is the Holy Spirit of God. The Son and the Spirit are different and separate states and parts, of the complete God. Both these are very special, but it is the Son who is coming as man's promised Messiah.

Advent means coming and we do not want to miss God's coming, but we want to be ready for it and to share in it. So today, as we are aroused by the watchmen, we need to celebrate with God, Jesus, the Holy Spirit and our fellow watchmen and so alert others to this wonderful event to come. As Christians our awareness is stirred now, and we thank God that He has not forgotten us, and that we can see Him coming to us now, if we look with the watchmen. The watchmen wake us up now, and tell us the Messiah is coming. So we can be ready and go to look for and to meet Him, even as He comes to us. They point us in the right direction so we too can see the Messiah coming. During this Advent we learn about why God came to the world as this special part of Himself, to be our Saviour. So now we must be alert and watchful. We need to be worthy watchmen. Watchmen are dedicated observers and are often the first ones to see changes happening. Of course they then have to react to the changes they see, and here we see they sing for joy, as they are happy to see the Lord coming and their joy shows others the Lord is coming. They share their experience, of seeing the coming of God, with one another and this means others can share this too. In this book throughout Advent, we will see how God shares Himself and His blessings to all men and we are similarly called to share our blessings (and in fact ourselves) with God and all other peoples. The watchmen are happy because they know the Lord God is good and brings good things for all to share in. This really is something to have high hopes and expectations for, God coming to be with us.

In a short while we will be celebrating the birth of Jesus Christ, God's Son and our Messiah. Jesus the Messiah came to lead us to God forever. We must be watchful for the arrival and return of the Lord Jesus, but we should also be watchful to see that the enemy, the Devil, does not assault us. The Devil does not want people to be with God, and tries to discredit God, by leading man from God. Isaiah points to the coming of the Messiah, who Christians now believe, came about two thousand years ago, and who also believe that He will return again. When Jesus the Messiah comes again it will be judgement day, at which, the enemy, Satan and his powers of evil and followers, will be banished forever to reside in Hell only, eternally cut off from, and unable to be and share with the Lord in His heavenly kingdom. The watchmen need to recognise good from bad, truth from lies, and to do this they need to be wise, and responsible as mentioned already. The watchmen in the Old Testament include the leaders of Israel, (the Jewish nation, from Abraham to David), the prophets and many of the other characters featured therein. The watchmen in the Advent story of the New Testament include Mary and Joseph, Mary's cousin Elizabeth and her husband Zechariah, and the shepherds, and all who were aware of the imminent birth and significance of Jesus. Shortly after Advent, and Jesus' birth, the Wise Men, Simeon, and John the Baptist acted as watchmen. We need watchmen today in our society and lives, to look out for the second Advent, and we hope that some of our Christian Church leaders are fulfilling this role.

The amazing fact of Jesus is that at the same time He is both man and a part of God. He is the Son of Man and the Son of God. The son is not greater than or equal to the father but is in fact a unique and special part and extension of the father (similar, but different). God creates Jesus to be His Son, solely to be our Saviour. Jesus is Messiah and Saviour. This is God's plan to save man, through this special part of Himself that we can relate to. Jesus is God's wonderful gracious gift to us. Jesus is a marvellous gift of love to us from God. Jesus as a man could fully relate to all the experiences of a man, but as the Son of God had an understanding of God and divine experience, that no human could ever have. These qualities made for an ideal Messiah, able to understand and interact, between God and man.

Originally God gave His blessing to Abraham and made a promise that He would look after Abraham's descendants if they continued to love and obey God. These people became the Jewish nation and they believed through their scriptures (the Word of God, given to and proclaimed by the prophets and written on scrolls known as the Torah) that God would send an anointed one to them to help them, the Messiah. Why did man need a Messiah? The problem of man's sin is too great to be solved by man alone. Man needs God to help him deal with man's sin. The Jews tried many leaders for their nation to follow God. Some were successful, but only in the short term, and others were even less successful! Special help from God was needed and this was to come in the form of the Messiah, who as we have already said, would conquer over man's sin and so lead man back to God. While the Jews believed the Messiah was to come and would be anointed by God, some did not believe He would in fact be God's own Son. Later others acknowledged Jesus as the Messiah (notably Peter, see Mark 8 v29), though many then could not also believe that while being the Son of Man, Jesus the Messiah was also the Son of God. This certainly remains the same today, and proves a barrier to belief in Jesus as the Messiah, to many people.

So we can think of each Advent as the time two thousand years ago before Jesus' birth when the Jews were eagerly awaiting their Messiah to come to help them. We know now how mistaken some of them were with their beliefs that the Messiah would end Roman rule immediately, and lead the Jewish nation only. How difficult it is to be exactly sure of God's purposes but the theme through the Old Testament is to worship God alone and to obey the commandments He gave as His covenant with Moses for the Jewish people. To ascribe more into God's work is very dangerous ground, but one which many have fallen into the trap of doing so over the years. Isaiah prophesies about the coming of the Messiah, and later we read his other prophecies that point to Jesus being this Messiah. Whilst we are now looking forward to the birth of the Messiah, Jesus, at this Advent season, we are fortunate to also already know about the life and ministry of Jesus the Messiah. At Advent now it is helpful for us to look back in the Old Testament and then to look forward as it were, in the New Testament, to find out all we can about the Messiah God promised man. In doing this we know of Jesus' ministry that showed Him to be the Messiah and how He conquered sin and has led man back to God. Isaiah and the Old Testament prophets did not know the details that we now do about Jesus the Messiah and especially how He fulfilled His Messianic ministry. However as we will see from the Advent readings His birth, life and death were prophesied in the Old Testament, and these prophecies were fulfilled by the Jesus of the New Testament. This early prophecy about the Messiah, coupled with the later details of Jesus' life, helps affirm that Jesus was the promised Messiah. This will be referred to later through these daily readings.

We can also think of each Advent in our own times. We sometimes wonder why Jesus came when He did and not into our modern world, but are we any better as people for having all the modern technological advances that we have now compared to then? Perhaps we are worse off as people intrinsically. We must have as much cause for hope at this time today, as at both the periods Isaiah lived in and as at that very first Advent time, before Jesus' birth in Bethlehem. In some ways the time and the place of the Advent story are slightly irrelevant, what really matters is mainly the actual event and a good understanding of it. Today we are privileged to know more about Jesus than in the years before He came to earth and then returned to heaven, and we know of God's love for all men and that Jesus brings salvation for all men, not just the Jewish nation. Man now has had time to study God's word of the Old and New Testaments and to try and understand it and apply it to life. So now we hope for God's kingdom to come on earth as it is in heaven, as one day this will surely happen. Meanwhile we can ensure and play our part in bringing God's kingdom to earth, by making our hearts, minds, souls and bodies to be fitting places (temples) for God and His kingdom. When the kingdom fully comes, Jesus will come again and we look forward eagerly to His Second Coming and the next part of our Christian story. We now should be watchmen for the second and final coming of Jesus. We are told in the New Testament of what to look for that will point to that event.

Meanwhile the Advent preparation has now started and should go on and can be likened to training before a race. Daily, we hope to, and can get closer to God, and by many means we can help to achieve this (meditating and praying, fasting and praising in our work and relaxation). Whatever we do, we must honour God in all we do, during this Advent time, and beyond. Also we need to tell all people about Jesus and that He is the way to God in the new covenant (agreement) God has given to us through His Son Jesus.

In Advent in our church there are traditions practised such as special candles lit during Advent. One is lit each Sunday of Advent in a circle and one in the centre for the birth of Jesus on Christmas Day. The outer candles can symbolise hope, love, joy and peace and are often red or pink, with the centre one white. They represent the light of God burning brightly and lighting any dark places. God, Jesus and the Holy Spirit will light the dark places and bring life to them. Life struggles in the darkness and chaos and sin can occur easily and go unnoticed generally, but the struggles and chaos and sin are lessened by the light, which brings order and right to life more easily. In Anglican churches, the altar cloth and priests' vestments may be changed to the colour purple, the Advent colour (purple is meant to signify richness and royalty). These are changed to white at Christmas. We will have carols (songs and hymns about Christmas) and other special Church services and activities, to heighten our awareness of this time. These include carol services, services of readings and carols, Christingle services and nativity services. Groups of musicians and singers often go from house to house, singing carols to the community. This is a type of evangelism, especially if they invite people to come to services at their churches; hoping to give them a chance to join the Church and come to God. Often people will also give money as a donation to the church or group they represent, in exchange for being entertained by their singing. In the secular world there are films (White Christmas etc), books (Dickens' Christmas Carol), art and crafts, pop songs, music concerts and plays. Also, Christmas Day and the day after, are Bank Holidays, which are national public holidays for most people. Many others including the schools take holidays over this time. All these practices imply a change and so mark this as a different special season.

In England we are midway through our winter and are used to images of Christmas wintry scenes, whereas in Southern Hemisphere countries Christmas time occurs at midsummer. Jesus was born in the Middle East in Bethlehem, which would probably have been cold and dark. Other Advent and Christmas traditions include Advent calendars and Advent and Christmas cards and decorations. Many of these items are meant to be symbolic and representative of the biblical Christian story (angels, star, etc). These calendars generally do not correlate their start with Advent Sunday, instead they usually start from the first day of December. The Advent calendars have hidden pictures or characters, which are revealed daily and are witnesses to God in our daily lives. They culminate on the twenty fifth of December with baby Jesus. Many people, both Christians and non Christians, though also decorate with non Christian images and icons (Reindeers, Santa Claus etc) and the Advent story can become mixed up, confused and even lost. Decorations are put inside and outside homes and buildings. Many have illuminations, which are switched on in the evenings to shine out in, and light up, the dark evenings and nights. Christmas trees are placed inside and outside and are also decorated with lights and other items. Advent wreaths are common and many craft items are made as decorations. Some of these may be carved or manufactured nativity sets or secular non Christmas items e.g. Santas and reindeers. Candles (wax or electric) are placed in windows and lit. The decorations are intended to cheer people up, lights in the darkness signifying welcome and warmth and God's presence in the darkness and to alert them to the special event ahead. Streets in villages, towns and cities are decorated in this way. With the right intent and use, these can help in our spiritual preparation at this time, helping us to focus on God and share this special time with others.

Nativity plays are popular at this time especially for young children in schools, to help them enjoy and remember the Advent story. It is thought that Saint Francis of Assisi was the first to bring nativity scenes into Church and many churches continue this example. Another custom is constructing a Jesse tree. This stems (pun!) from Jesus' relation to David, honoured king of Israel, whose father was Jesse and is in effect a representation of Jesus' earthly family tree. The branches can hold reminders of Jesus and the Advent story, and often have a Bible text on. Jesse trees have been done to collect items for charity with these placed on each of the twenty-five branches and given to charity around Christmas Day.

The start of Advent then is the time Christians start to prepare for Christmas. The secular world has no official time to start Christmas preparations. Many shops display Christmas goods and services (holidays, entertainments etc) much earlier than the first day of Advent. Many manufacturers are busy year round making items solely for the Advent and Christmas period. This is big business. However, the secular preparations leading to Christmas Day often do not encourage proper spiritual preparation with manufacturers and retailers trying to boost trade and sales purely for profit. Profit itself is not necessarily bad, if it is used for the glory of God. If it is not though, it does become a problem. Through many media areas, we are encouraged to go for Christmas meals, to buy questionable presents and join the crowded shoppers. Many write and send Christmas greeting cards and many plan family gatherings. These need extra catering arrangements and special Advent and Christmas food is obtained and prepared. For example, Christmas cake, Christmas puddings, mincepies are all traditionally made and eaten at this time. Too much activity and preparation on peripheral matters leaves people tired and unable to concentrate on the central issue of the coming birth of Jesus. Let us put all non essential matters aside at this time, and be guided by God in remembering Mary and Joseph awaiting and participating in the special birth of Jesus (which was much more so than even a normal birth which is special).

Another Jewish prophet from the Old Testament, Jeremiah (Jer.10 v3), gave a warning to the Israelites in exile in Babylon to beware following the pagan example of the Babylonians of decorating trees and worshipping those and other icons and false gods. He was urging the Jews to keep their own traditions of celebrating with the one true God and not to lose sight of God by worshipping idols and we need to be aware of that. Do we have a fairy at the top of the Christmas tree or is it an angel of God? Or is it a representation of baby Jesus, which we can focus on, or is it an unrecognizable bauble or idol? Let us take care we honour God with both our traditions and actions. We need to attend to our spiritual sustenance and rest, and we can do this by reading God's Word in the Bible, by praying and praising and helping those around us.

Now is an opportune time to think of our families and also the wider family of God's people. Family life has been an important aspect to God. He created Adam and Eve to start the family of man, to make family life part of man's existence. God strengthened this with the fifth commandment and with the importance He gives to all ages and states of family life (to children, elderly, singles, couples, widows and divorcees). We need to pray that God can be honoured in all families, and not ignored or worse despised. This Advent hope comes to a broken sinful world, which we pray it will help heal. We know it can do this, but that in some cases this is not an easy process, and may involve pain, before healing occurs. We pray our hope and joy will sustain us through any trials to come and that we can rejoice in our Advent hope, whether we are in difficulty and despair or we are in ease and enthralment. We can take this time as a starting point which has changed the world, but we need to accept this with our belief in God.

So we have high hopes at this time, which need to rise and be sustained until Christmas Day and beyond. As today is the start of the Church's New Year, Happy New Year!

Further reading - 1 Thessalonians 5 v1- 11.

Prayer - Lord God, we eagerly await Your coming. Keep us alert, and help us prepare and be ready for Your arrival.

Action - (Suggestion - prayer and praise using any appropriate activity- use your imagination!).

Notes -

Advent 1 Monday (1/2)
The Hope of the coming Messiah Jesus

<u>Isaiah 1 v21-26 (RSV).</u> *How the faithful city has become a harlot, she that was full of justice! Righteousness lodged in her, but now murderers. Your silver has become dross, your wine mixed with water. Your princes are rebels and companions of thieves. Everyone loves a bride and runs after gifts. They do not defend the fatherless and the widow's cause does not come to them. Therefore the Lord says, the Lord of Hosts, the Mighty One of Israel, "Ah I will rent my wrath on my enemies and avenge myself on my foes. I will turn my hand against you and will smelt away your dross as with lye and remove all your alloy. And I will restore all your judges as at the first, and your counsellors as at the beginning. Afterward you shall be called the city of righteousness, the faithful city".*

In this reading, Isaiah reminds us why we need God. Man is sinful and cannot live fully without God. Many people have grown away from God and wrongdoing has resulted. Mankind needs a return to righteousness and we hope God will help us be restored to righteousness. Isaiah continues the theme of God's holy place on earth stating that it has fallen badly into disrepute and is in need of restoration. Even God's chosen place, (which is the city of Jerusalem), for His dwelling on earth is corrupted by men.

The Lord God will judge all men and His enemies He will severely punish. God says the leaders and people have become shallow and much worse, thieves, murderers. They do not help the helpless. God knows that men are sinful but those who repent and turn and love Him will be saved from the punishment of being separated from God, His love and blessing. God is a loving Father, but even His patience is not without limit to those who have, and who continue to consciously deny Him. He will not let the wicked prosper and the righteous suffer forever. We know the Lord will come and now we know He will restore His way of justice when He does. Some sins are worse than others, and the Old Testament writers tell us the worst sin is purposefully sinning against God. Jesus in the New Testament reiterates this, saying the worst sin is deliberately sinning against the Holy Spirit (Mat 12v 30-32). It seems that in the Old Testament, God was very severe in dealing with the wicked and that this message has been redirected by Jesus' teachings in the New Testament. Jesus the Messiah tells us that we must leave judgement and punishment up to God, and that we need to show mercy and forgiveness to the wicked as God shows this to us and all people. The Old Testament though seems to have two themes running side by side. Firstly God's love for His faithful people and secondly His retribution for the unfaithful people. Jesus came stressing God's love for all mankind, and that all who truly repent will receive God's love. If we repent sincerely God will forgive us. We need to be sincere and to make efforts to cast our sin aside. It can be hard to obey God's Commandments but the rewards can be tremendous satisfaction in doing so, unlike sinful living where the rewards are often unsatisfying, hollow and empty. God may act as a loving father who rightly punishes the wrongdoings of His people, as a loving father applying his discipline to his own children. If God did not do so we would suffer from being ill disciplined, immature and spoilt and that would not enable us to reach the true potential God wants for every one of us. There is a strong theme in the Old Testament of the people continually turning from God and provoking Him to anger with the need for Him to bring on His people punishment or discipline.

It is a great comfort to know that God sees the actions of the wicked and will not let them prevail forever. We have our hope in His promise that He will restore righteous leaders and good order will be restored. God yearns for us to live good lives and He will help us to achieve that. This was God's marvellous promise to the people of Isaiah's time and still is His promise to us now.

Jerusalem at this time of the Advent story was a city under foreign, Roman, occupation. This seemed a long way away from the time of David and Solomon when the Jews had rebuilt it to be the place for God to stay with the Ark of the Covenant, and Temple and religious practices were done to honour God. The Jews were hoping for God's return and the restoration of Jerusalem (back to the good old days, but those days demand respect for and obedience to God). At this time the Romans worshipped their own gods and especially held their leader, called Emperor, to be a god himself. They called for all the people they conquered to follow their traditions and often they despised the local peoples own beliefs and gods. Later though some Roman leaders became converts to Christianity, and many years later Rome, the capital of the Roman Empire became the site of the Roman Church, later known as the Roman Catholic Church. The leader became the Holy Roman Emperor, a Christian, and a Christian person was appointed as chief priest in charge of the Church based in Rome, but spread through the Roman Empire. This priest was titled Pope, and the office of Pope is still in existence now, as the head of the Roman Catholic Church today.

Returning to Advent, if the Messiah is coming now are we ready for Him? While we watch for God's coming we must not just be staring and have preconceived notions of how and when He comes. If instead we are open (our eyes, ears, hearts, minds and whole body) we can see and experience God all around us, even in the unlikeliest of places. As Christians we must ourselves reflect God's glory and be prepared to proclaim Him publicly. This is a tall order though we have to try and tackle it if our faith is to mean anything real for God, the world and ourselves. Let us try not to fall from God's way at this special Advent time of year when we can easily become distracted and lose our way to and from God.

To help us at this time if we plan our secular and spiritual activities we are more likely to carry them through. Also and most importantly, we should ensure our preparations will glorify God in a fitting manner rather than be simply pleasing to ourselves. If we have not been wholly satisfied with previous Advent and Christmas seasons, we should make allowances now so that we do not repeat previous errors this year. Our plans may include presents to buy for family and friends. These presents represent the gifts brought to the baby Jesus by the shepherds and Wise Men. It is not known if the shepherds gave any gifts as the Wise Men did, but they certainly gave their time to honour the Messiah with. Over Advent and Christmas we may need to make travel and accommodation arrangements for family, guests or ourselves and plans for the holiday ahead. We may wish to plan decorations and the Christmas cards to exchange, communicating good will greetings and hopefully to proclaim Jesus' birth. Also we may want to check food and drink, to try to make a special celebration meal with traditional seasonal fare for Jesus's birthday on Christmas Day. As Christians we need to share our experience of, and intended plans for, this Advent and Christmas season with as many people as we can, especially with those who either have not come to Jesus and who have less to share than we have.

In the UK we tend to think of this season as our traditional Northern Hemisphere Advent and Christmas time in contrast to the warmer Southern Hemisphere time. When I lived and worked in Cyprus I participated in a local tradition with work colleagues of a swim in the sea before Church on Christmas Day. This was bracing, but fun, though I have never done this in UK, as it would be far too cold in the sea! I'm sure in many southern hemisphere countries, a swim before Church, whether in the sea or outdoor pools is probably quite usual, and sounds pleasant to me, but I personally have never celebrated Christmas in any such place or during midsummer. One day, perhaps

I might be fortunate to experience Advent and Christmas in the southern hemisphere! This leads us on to thinking how the Christian faith has spread out from Bethlehem on that first Advent to reach all parts of the world and for us to appreciate that Advent and Christmas is truly for all people worldwide to prepare for and to celebrate.

Further reading - Romans 13 v8-end.

Prayer - Lord, we pray for Your justice in the world, and that You will be honoured in every part of the world.

Action -

Notes -

Advent 1 Tuesday (1/3)
The Hope of the coming Messiah Jesus

<u>Isaiah 2 v2-4 (GNB).</u> *In days to come the mountain where the temple stands will be the highest one of all, towering above all the hills. Many nations will come streaming to it, and their people will say "Let us go up the hill of the Lord, to the temple of Israel's God. He will teach us what he wants us to do; we will walk in the paths He has chosen. For the Lord's teaching comes from Jerusalem; from Zion He speaks to His people. He will settle disputes among great nations. They will hammer their swords into ploughs and their spears into pruning knives. Nations will never again go to war, never prepare for battle again."*

Isaiah tells us here of what great things God will do for His people, and that God will return again to the Temple in Jerusalem. This will be His dwelling on earth and when that happens all people will recognise this and will come and learn from Him and honour Him there. This will lead to the ultimate reward of peace. Isaiah emphasizes that the way to peace is through obeying God.

Peace, what a marvellous hope to aspire to and to be promised to us. The end to physical suffering and psychological pain too. The Lord has promised this and declares that He is the God of peace. Throughout history man has fought wars despite God's commandment not to kill and the Christian message that it is sinful to kill. God creates us for His purpose and it is a sin for another man to purposefully end some other person's God-given life. It is also generally a sin to take your own life, as this is not part of the purpose God gave us life. The exception being if anyone lays down his life for the life of someone else as directed by God. Jesus of course, was an example of this as He in effect gave His life for everyone, under God's instruction. Jesus though was an exception as He was fulfilling His Messianic mission by doing this, and no one else is called by God to do such a thing again. Killing and wars are often brought on by sinful motives (aggression, greed) so to have an end to killing and war would mean the sinful motives behind these acts would be conquered and controlled. Unfortunately though, even now, two thousand years after Jesus' life and death there are wars happening around the world in many countries. Jesus said this would be the case, but we must try to do anything and all we can to stop killing and war, as these often needlessly destroy people and property, and much of the environment, a tragic loss and waste of precious life and resources. There are many reasons for wars and killing, even including reasons of religion, (shown especially today in Muslim Northern Sudan against Christian southern Sudan). There are wars to end oppressive unjust regimes and wars started by countries to gain power and territory. Presently we face a worldwide war waged by terrorists from many places who kill innocent people to bring attention to their concerns, and possibly hoping to gain power and change, by force and fear. This is cowardly and ungodly. There have been wars to remove races and cultures from the world. All involve pain and destruction and are not an acceptable and responsible way to solve man's problems and differences. In the last resort God has helped His people in war, though only in the most extreme case and when the enemy have been sinful and provoking God (as when Joshua fought at Jericho and the other battles to give the Jews the Promised Land). In contrast, God has allowed wars to occur as an extreme measure of His judgement to wicked people, including His original chosen and favoured Jewish people, when they have been unfaithful to God.

Overall God wants the best for all people, and that means peace between all people. Here Isaiah says at the time when God is acknowledged supreme (when the Temple towers over all) many nations will come to God for instruction and peace. God is not just for the Jews, but for all nations. I believe this may be a time when all nations recognize the importance of and aspire to attaining Christian beliefs. What a wonderful hope that would be. In contrast to war, peace however builds people and property. War can bring out hatred whereas peace can bring love. Only if we have proper peace at home can we hope to spread peace abroad. There are many challenges and diversions to peace at home and as Christians we must work for love and peace between our friends and neighbours and enemies. During the First World War trench warfare hostilities ceased on Christmas Day but then resumed at the same intensity the next day. That day, Jesus the Messiah brought a brief moment of peace to the horror of battle, where Christian nations and men fought and killed one another instead of resolving the conflict peacefully. The next day though Jesus was set aside and forgotten and the war raged again.

To obtain peace we must obey God's Commandments daily, and Jesus helps us get close to God which is where we need to be, to be sure we are doing God's will. Presently, in UK, we are reducing our own armed forces personnel and we hope that those that once bore arms can now make peaceful tools and redundant weaponry be recycled for peaceful purposes. World peace is a dream we must strive to make a reality and worldwide Christian principles and love are the main hope for this to happen. Jesus never advocated violence or aggression as a means to achieve any progress. He did cause a stir in the Temple by turning over the tax collectors and sacrifice sellers' tables, but didn't intend to physically hurt them. He did tell His followers that they would have to endure violence and aggression themselves and that they should be strong enough to endure this and should also be able to forgive their enemies. Jesus the Messiah proclaimed the importance of peace and that the way to it is through love of both God and man. Jesus emphasised we must love all men including our enemies in order to gain the peace and love of God in our lives and in the world. As we await the birth of Jesus, we can think of this small baby in whom there was no wish to harm people and who was free of sin. It sometimes seems a shame that all of us grow from innocent babies and become more affected by sin.

For us to be at peace with others we need to be at peace with ourselves and more importantly with God, Jesus and the Holy Spirit. Often during Holy Communion in a Church service we offer one another a greeting saying the peace of the Lord God be with you. We need to offer this peace to all we meet in our daily lives as well as to pray to God for His peace to come on earth. Also the peace of God, as well as bringing an end to actual physical conflict and war will also bring an end to spiritual and psychological war, resulting in complete peace. The peace of God will be present anywhere and everywhere and especially to be within people's hearts and minds. As Christians, we fully believe in a peaceful eternal life, which we can now reach thanks to Jesus conquering over sin and death.

Here Isaiah emphasises the restoration and restitution of Jerusalem. God will dwell again in His Temple there, and it will be a place respected by many great nations. This is a phenomenal hope, that all men and nations will recognise the authority and sovereignty of God and that they will come to Him to solve their problems and will honour and respect Him. It is a hope that is realised through Jesus, and one day will be a reality that all people can share in, through belief in Jesus, Son of God. Jerusalem is a city that has been fought over for many years. It was the place David captured and rebuilt as the capital of the kingdom of Israel. It was the place chosen where the Ark of the Covenant came and where God was to be worshipped, and later the Temple was to be built. Since then, it has been claimed by many people of different cultures and faiths, and it is thought to be where God's heavenly kingdom will eventually be established when Jesus returns at His second coming. Isaiah knows the Jews have a central role to play in honouring God, but he also knows that all other people can honour God and can share in God's love. It will be wonderful when this prophecy is achieved and all men can live peacefully in

Jerusalem with one another and with God being honoured in the Temple there, and all over the world.

Further reading - Romans 5 v1.

Prayer - Lord, thank You for Your power, wisdom and knowledge and love. May we grow with you each day. We pray for Your peace to be over the entire world and especially in the hearts of all men.

Action -

Notes -

Advent 1 Wednesday (1/4)
The Hope of the coming Messiah Jesus

<u>Matthew 13 v44-45 (RSV).</u> *The kingdom of heaven is like treasure hidden in a field which a man found and covered up; then in his joy he goes and sells all that he has and buys that field.*

Today's reading is from the Gospel of Matthew in the New Testament, and is about Jesus telling of the kingdom of heaven. This is God's full eternal kingdom, which is different to, but it also includes and encompasses God's kingdom on earth. God's creation includes heaven and earth and Jesus the Messiah and Saviour bridges the gulf between heaven and earth. This heaven is not the sky, stars and space above the earth, but is the dimension God exists in and from which He made the universe. Jesus is heavenly as Son of God, and earthly as Son of Man, and He proclaims God's glory in both these kingdoms. We have our own direct experience of the earth and we can make certain sure predictions about that. God made the earth and also man, to enjoy both, though they are only a part of God's whole creation. God made the whole universe, and may even have made heaven. We know much less about these matters and we certainly know less about heaven than earth. Jesus the Messiah tells us something of heaven and again it is described in other books of the Old and New Testaments. Again, we need to make our own minds up based on this information and our own insight, knowledge, wisdom and in the end, belief. So, I believe heaven is where God exists fully, and where man can be with Him fully and eternally. Most Christians believe that God transcends heaven and earth although it can be difficult to describe God and His realm of heaven. The Bible also states though, when God comes, His kingdom will come also. God the King comes with His heavenly kingdom established, and a new earthly kingdom will be created. Jesus came to start the process of re-establishing God's kingdom on earth and He will return again when this has been fully achieved.

Jesus tells us in the reading here, how wonderful heaven is. He describes it as a treasure that is both wonderful and irresistible and has no equal. This treasure is wonderful and eternal. It does not decay or perish, but is of eternal, everlasting, wonderful value. Jesus tells us what to do when we find it, so we can possess it forever. However to attain it we have to do something, and that means giving up some of what we already have, so that we can obtain the far greater richness that this treasure is, in comparison to our own effects. Jesus, in fact, says here that it is worth giving up all we have in order to gain the richest treasure of the kingdom of heaven. It also shows that we need to possess heaven lawfully and cannot take it by stealing or any other means. Once it is found it needs to be looked after to prevent it being stolen and so lost, until it is possessed legally and fully. However, we all have to put our own interpretation on the kingdom of heaven and I believe it to be where we can and will be directly with God.

Presently here on earth we have God's Spirit with us, the Holy Spirit. We see God's works all around us but we are not in direct contact with God, as Adam and Eve were in the Garden of Eden. We are separated from God by our sinful nature. Jesus has broken the power of that sin for us. So that, if we believe in, and act for Jesus, then we can come to God knowing our sin is forgiven and dealt with by Jesus who died for us, to take our sin away, allowing us to get back to God. Now not even death can separate us from God, for Jesus rose to life again after dying a terribly cruel death for every single person who has lived and for who is yet to live. Through following Jesus Christ we can now come to, and be with, God eternally and so gain the gift of eternal life. We do not know when we may be called to, or find heaven, or when God and the kingdom of heaven may come and be established on the earth, but we can look forward to each of these events. Heaven then is being with God, Jesus and the Holy Spirit and we can find such a place here on earth if we are very fortunate and blessed, in our hearts and in the hearts of others. Some Jews still wait for a Messiah to come and rebuild the Temple in Jerusalem, however Jesus came as Messiah to make the hearts of men fitting places for God, so building a living Temple for God (known to Christians as the Church). When all men have God, Jesus and the Holy Spirit in their hearts, then I believe Jesus will return again to earth with the kingdom of God, and as God has promised Jerusalem will be the capital of God's kingdom on earth. For now, there is also such a place of heaven in God's other dimension, in His eternal kingdom where He resides with the angels and heavenly beings including Jesus.

This passage shows that this heaven is hidden and needs to be discovered, and is well worth searching out. It is possible to find such a thing by accident or by intent, though once we find it we become changed, and realise its importance and value. Heaven is like this treasure, an undeserved blessing, that man has not made but has been provided with and is there to be found, available for anyone to find and possess. This extraordinary treasure of heaven is present within an ordinary place and some effort is needed firstly to find it and recognize it and then secondly, to keep it. Jesus tells us in this passage what a good thing Heaven is. As we thank God for this knowledge, we must thank God for our daily lives which are also very wonderful, no matter what joy or pain we are experiencing right now. Life is special, whether or not some people have dire hardships, and others do not have such difficulties. Wherever on that spectrum we are, we should remember, life is a God given gift and so is attaining the kingdom of heaven. We cannot achieve either by our own efforts. In heaven the problems of our own earthly lives will be truly behind us and we will be fully with and wholly in God's loving care. We read of the faith we must have to reach the kingdom of heaven throughout the Bible and here in this passage. We have to be fully committed to God, so much so that we will give up all that we have with the firm belief that this will bring us to the kingdom. Can we imagine being like that man who has a glimpse of heaven and then goes all out to get there too? We get glimpses of heaven throughout our lives and we need to be alert to these and not waste any of these opportunities. Believing in God and doing God's will is sometimes hard, but it is always fulfilling and rewarding and the treasure of heaven will be the ultimate final reward for doing this.

So to gain these riches, we must spend time with and love God. This time will help make us grow and bear fruit and this will encourage and influence the world and heaven around us. We cannot let ourselves grow but not bear fruit. So let us think how we can bear fruit for the Lord God. We need to do this now here on earth and with the gift of eternal life we can continue this later in heaven also. All this is available to all people through Jesus, who we are waiting for now and who is coming to us soon, on Christmas Day. We pray that our fruit bearing will be continual and appropriate. We must not produce a poor crop if we are capable of better things. The New Testament says that from those who have much, much will be expected. Everyone is different but we are all capable of bearing this fruit for the Lord God if we ask Him and let Him guide us appropriately. We look forward to doing this here and now, and eternally in Heaven.

Further reading - Matthew 25 v31-end.

Prayer - Lord God, we thank You for being with us now in Your Spirit, and that we will later be with You fully in heaven. Help us both to give up, and to take up what we need to, in order to be with You, now and always.

Action -
Notes -

Advent 1 Thursday (1/5)
The Hope of the coming Messiah Jesus

1 Thessalonians 2 v13 (RSV). *And we also constantly thank God for this, that when you received the word of God which you heard from us you accepted it not as the word of men, but as what it really is, the word of God which is at work in you believers.*

Today's reading, is from the Apostle Paul, from the New Testament, and reminds us that the Holy Spirit gives us the Word of God through Jesus' followers. We must look to our leaders of present and past to hear the Word of God. Next week in Advent two, we celebrate with the Word of God in the Old Testament from the prophets. The apostle Paul praises the Thessalonians for he sees that God's Word is being used by them and is at work amongst them. This is what we all must aim for, remembering from yesterday's reading, that God's Word with us, will work within us to bear fruit. We do not want to fall into the traps that are set around us, to be hypocritical in our faith as Jesus called many of the Pharisees and Sadducees (pious, strict, Jewish religious sects). We should not hear the Word of God and not be changed by it. We should let it work in us to develop ourselves as better people, bringing us to God, Jesus and the Holy Spirit. We definitely ought not to reject the Word of the Lord God. The people who do reject the Word of God will not share in God's eternal kingdom unless they repent and ask for forgiveness. Others who hear the Word of God, but don't let it affect their lives will be unfulfilled and when ultimately judged by God, consequently may not be given a share in God's eternal kingdom. We all must rejoice however that God has through Jesus, made Himself available to anyone who wishes to know Him and receive his eternal love and blessing. The Father will love anyone who believes in and loves His Son.

Jesus comes as the promised Messiah the Jews await, but more importantly God has opened Himself to all people if they believe in Him through His Son, Jesus, and the Holy Spirit. We need faith to believe these things, and to do the work the word of God calls us to do. We need to encourage and support one another in this, and we need courage to let go fully of ourselves and give ourselves to God so that He will work fully through us. Let us let go, and let God, rule our lives. So let us be transformed by God so that first and foremost in our lives we live for and with God. He will lead each one of us to our proper place and role in life and will let us fulfil ourselves properly if we will just fully let Him into our lives. We all have different duties, skills and abilities and different talents to give to God. We must all encourage one another to spread the word of God to non believers, as well as encouraging all growth from present believers. We need to study the words of Paul, in his New Testament writing, the Jew, who originally persecuted Christians, but who later was converted by God to be a marvellous Christian witness. Paul later was killed for his belief in Jesus, and after was made a saint by the Christian Church.

Jesus is the Word of God made flesh (incarnate). Jesus spoke the word of God throughout His life and ministry, to His disciples, and to all those He met. Jesus was also the Word of God in action. The people Jesus encountered remembered the words and actions of Jesus, and discussed them among themselves and with others. Some of them wrote Jesus' words and actions down, and these are detailed in the books of the New Testament. The Word of God should result in the action of God and in Jesus we have the perfect example of this. Jesus is the example of leading a God centred life we should follow. Paul himself tries to follow Jesus' example, and Paul encourages others to do this too. All these people then have been affected by the Advent time that resulted in the birth of Jesus. They inspire us today to follow their example to hear and apply the word of God in our lives.

Advent, is now a good time to have Christian group activity. We can use the imminent birth of Jesus to help us refocus on and redevelop our faith. We can have different church services at this time. Carol services as a means of praise and thanksgiving are popular. A service of lesson readings and carols has become a good way to combine the word of God with singing His praise. Some churches hold Christingle services. A Christingle is a representation of the world and God, in the shape of a decorated fruit (an orange or apple or similar). The fruit has a candle in the centre representing the light of God, and four sticks representing the compass points of the earth. These have raisins or sweets on representing the fruits of the earth. Around the middle of the fruit, a red ribbon is tied representing the blood of Jesus. We use this object to remind ourselves of what is of real importance, it can feed and sustain us and is a representation of what we need to give thanks to God for. We can participate in other group activities. Just as antenatal classes are given to prepare parents to be, about birth and parenthood to follow, and can be helpful and practical, Advent study groups can be practical and good at this time of year. It is good to share in a group with others, both in and out of church, studying and applying the word of God in relation to Advent and Christmas. Use a group activity like this, or any similar group activity, to bring the Word of God to those who have not experienced it and who do not know the meaning of Advent, and also to strengthen and refresh those who already know something of God and this Advent time. Share experiences and testimonies of Jesus in your own life with others.

Further reading - Psalm 130.

Prayer - Lord, we thank You for the praise, inspiration and works of Your servants. Thank You for Your Word in the Bible, may it inspire us also to honour You fittingly every day of our lives.

Action -

Notes -

Advent 1 Friday (1/6)
The Hope of the coming Messiah Jesus

<u>Isaiah 44 v2 (RSV).</u>   *Thus says the Lord who made you, who formed you from the womb and will help you: "Fear not O Jacob my servant, Jeshurun, whom I have chosen".*

Simply we are told not to be afraid, the Lord will help His chosen people. Isaiah is here encouraging the Jews again. This is wonderful, they did not need to be afraid of either the Lord God or anything else. When they are with God, there is nothing to fear because God has chosen them. This means there are no circumstances, either good ones or particularly bad ones to fear when God is with you. It is important to respect God, but not to be afraid of God. God can help anyone overcome any fear, even and especially fear of God Himself. Jacob was a son of Isaac, the son of Abraham, the founding father of the Jewish nation. Jacob was renamed Israel by God, when the Jews were in Egypt. Jeshurun is a Hebrew word meaning upright or righteous one. The Jewish people needed this encouragement because of the difficulties the Jewish nation were having at that time. Isaiah is firmly encouraging them by saying God will help them overcome all problems, and God promises them they should have no fears. This was a wonderful promise to the Jews at that time, as God was honouring His promise of help to them, His chosen people. The Jews were chosen because originally they honoured God, though later they fell away from righteous obedience and suffered God's judgement. Loving and obeying God leads to blessing, but dishonouring and disobeying God leads to discipline and punishment. Wonderfully through all these states God supports His chosen people, and will help deal with their fears.

We know that God loves all men whom He has created and we now believe this promise of help and encouragement applies to all who believe in God today. The Jews were awaiting the help God promised, a Messiah. We now know this Messiah has come, that He is Jesus, who we are preparing to meet on His coming birthday at Christmas. Jesus confirms that God no longer only favours the Jews, but His love is there for all who believe in Him and by believing in Him also believe in His Son Jesus and believe in God's Holy Spirit. Jesus, as Messiah, is the help God had promised to the Jews and is the Messiah and help for all people of all nations. To live without fear is marvellous, and can set us free to achieve our best for God. Fear is often thought of as being a necessary instinct, but it can stifle us if we let it. God gives us the chance to be without this potential burden if we trust in Him. We must let God help us to remove all our fears so that we can be His chosen people. Fear can be such a negative force that it can stifle our positive side if we let it. It is wonderful to know that God wants us to be without fear and will help us to achieve this aim.

Sadly the approach of Christmas does bring worry and fear to some people. There are many reasons today for that, but as Christians, we need to tell our neighbours that we have nothing to fear if we have God, Jesus and the Holy Spirit in our lives. It is probably impossible to remove the physiological side of fear from ourselves, but if we let God help us deal with the fear-producing events, we can be helped enormously. God will help us deal with fear, so that we do not become paralysed by it or a slave to it. Jesus the Messiah taught about not worrying, and now we must be watchful and hopeful and pray to God about Jesus' arrival at this Advent time. Now we think of Mary and Joseph, who were obedient to God. For them, obeying God seems to have been enough to have conquered any fears they may have had. They had a faith that allowed them to obey God, when He gave them this very special task. Whatever fear they may have had over this, they obeyed God and let Him deal with their fear and worries. Only with God's help did they fulfill their role and overcome the difficulties. They encountered much joy and difficulty, and later Mary especially faced much sorrow, but through it all they remained obedient to God, completing the task He had given them.

It is often said that God does not ask of His people more than they can endure, and that with God anything is possible, as Jesus proclaimed during His ministry. Mary and Joseph remain inspirational figures and examples to us today, with their faith in, and obedience to, God. We can also think of the disciples and apostles whose fears Jesus later took away. We also think of many people with whom Jesus met and gave them inner peace and removed their fears. We can think of these examples and of our own experiences to show others around us that fear is fruitless when we believe in God and Jesus and the Holy Spirit. In general fear leads to a negative life, which is not what God, Jesus and the Holy Spirit have planned for human life. How good it is not to be troubled, especially in this troubled world. The world seems full of stress and problems, though most are made worse by man's inappropriate actions, and all are made worse by being separated from God. It is good to bring our fears to the Lord Jesus, to both the crib and the cross to come. Living our lives as His servants we know of all the many temptations we face in life and the ease with which we can fall into sin. Yet we see in the Gospels how much more temptation Jesus Himself faced and how He overcame all of that with His resolute belief in God His Father. We must always strive to follow Jesus as our example, though when we do go wrong we can ask for and get forgiveness from God, Jesus and the Holy Spirit.

Further reading - Philippians 4 v6-7.

Prayer - Lord God, thank You for all Your help to us. Let our lives be to Your praise and glory, confident that You can remove any and all of our fears.

Action -

Notes -

Advent 1 Saturday (1/7)
The Hope of the coming Messiah Jesus

<u>Isaiah 44 v21-23 (RSV).</u>   *Remember these things, O Jacob and Israel, for you are my servant; I formed you, you are my servant; O Israel, you will not be forgotten by me. I have swept away your transgressions like a cloud, and your sins like mist; return to me for I have redeemed you. Sing, O Heavens, for the Lord has done it; shout, O depths of the earth; break forth into singing, O Mountains, O forest and every tree in it! For the Lord has redeemed Jacob, and will be glorified in Israel.*

Isaiah tells here of God's forgiveness to Israel. This is a marvellous act. The Israeli nation had been through many difficulties, often arising when they fell from correctly honouring God. God repeatedly promised to restore them and here Isaiah is telling the people that God will once again restore them. God delivered the Jews from the Egyptians and led them to His Promised Land. They didn't fully obey God even when He led them over the Red Sea and through the desert to the Promised Land. It took them forty years before they learnt obedience and honour to God before He finally led them into the Promised Land. Once there, they established themselves and later built the Temple at Jerusalem. However they fell away from obeying God again, and the Promised Land was split into two kingdoms. Isaiah lived in Jerusalem, in the southern part of the divided kingdom, in Judah. The northern kingdom, Israel, had already been conquered by the Assyrians, and the Jews were dispersed from the land. Some were taken to Ninevah, the capital of Assyria and most were badly treated. The southern kingdom, Judah, stayed intact some while longer, and this was the time that Isaiah lived and called the Jews to honour God, so that God would protect them. Eventually, Judah also was conquered but this time it was by the action of Nebuchanezzar of Babylon, and the Jews from there suffered similarly and were taken into exile.

This reading underlines, and highlights the thread during the first week of Advent that God will look after His chosen people, and that God does forgive the sins of the people, even though the sin is great. We read earlier in the week that God will judge the wicked and deal with them severely. However the good news is God will not let sin come between Him and His people forever. Here we see God once again calling His chosen people back to Him and forgiving their earlier sins. Only God has the power to deal with sin in this way. God can remove sin and its effects, and is showing through Isaiah and the other prophets that this sin will ultimately be dealt with by God's Messiah,

His Son. Some of the people may abandon God, but He will not abandon them and even nature will rejoice at the work of God, and God will once again be praised by, and in, His chosen land of Israel. Isaiah says God calls His people to Him, to enjoy His love and care, and now we need to hear God's call and respond to Him. Isaiah is the instrument God uses to call people to Him. Let us respond to this call from Isaiah, and pray to God to be with Him.

Let us celebrate God's love to us daily. God is with us and we need to acknowledge that to ourselves joyfully and to others. In today's reading we see that even the earth itself gives praise to God and reflects His glory of creation. God is here calling His chosen people to return to Him and this is their great hope that God would allow them back to His presence, by forgiving their sin. God tells Isaiah to tell the Jews to turn to Him again. What good news to hear, but did they hear and act on it? We know that many of them did not return to God. Now we must not be like those, instead let us hear God call us, and return to Him. We now know that this is the hope for all men and not just for the Jews. So now we along with the Jews, can look forward to being with God. With the Jews we also look for the coming Messiah. Now is the time to give thanks to God for all He has given us, especially for this coming of Jesus the Messiah and Saviour. Today, we have the advantage that now we also have the further knowledge of Jesus and the Holy Spirit with us from the word of God of the New Testament. We need to thank God for that, and we need to celebrate and praise God through our whole lives no matter what our circumstances at the moment, whether good or bad or in between. It is sometimes easy to think that people who have material possessions and wealth have an easy life and may have more to be thankful for than poor people. We do know, however, that some people with wealth may be unsatisfied in life and these are the people who often lack faith in God. In contrast, poorer people materially, may be richer in God's faith and be more satisfied and fulfilled people. Under either circumstance, either rich or poor, it may be difficult to find faith in God and to think there is anything to celebrate in life.

However, with faith in God we know we are completely provided for in body, mind and spirit, and this is a constant cause for celebration. Saint Paul told the Church that with God, Jesus and the Holy Spirit in his Christian life, he found contentment in whatever circumstances he experienced. We need to look on life as Christian people and honour God, Jesus and the Holy Spirit. Now we are getting ready to celebrate the coming of the Messiah in our churches and outside in the wider world. We must give thanks to God for His full creation and for the gift of His Son, Messiah and Saviour. Now we thank God for His great mercy shown to Israel, to whom He sent Jesus His Son the Messiah and who we are preparing to meet at the end of this Advent.

Further reading - Luke 21 v25-33.

Prayer - Lord God, we thank You for Your faithfulness and forgiveness to all people. Thank You for Your grace that You came to us in the form of Your Son, as a baby to fully experience human life, to grow up to love and care for us and to redeem our sins.

Action -

Notes -

Advent Week 2
Main theme: The Prophecy of the coming Messiah Jesus
ADVENT SUNDAY 2

<u>Luke 4 v14-21 (RSV)</u>. *And Jesus returned in the power of the Spirit into Galilee, and a report concerning him went out through all the surrounding country. And he taught in their synagogues, being glorified by all. And he came to Nazareth, where he had been brought up; and he went to the synagogue, as his custom was, on the sabbath day. And he stood up to read; and there was given to him the book of the prophet Isaiah. He opened the book and found the place where it was written, "The spirit of the Lord is upon me, because he has anointed me to preach good news to the poor. He has sent me to proclaim release to the captives and recovering of sight to the blind to set at liberty those who are oppressed to proclaim the acceptable year of the Lord". And he closed the book and gave it back to the attendant and sat down; and the eyes all in the synagogue were fixed on him. And he began to say to them, "Today this scripture has been fulfilled in your hearing".*

The paradox today is the chosen reading is from Luke's gospel in the New Testament, as most of the prophecies of the Messiah come from the Old Testament. However the incident described in this passage, clearly shows the importance of God's Word in the Old Testament and which Jesus speaks of in this reading. The writings of the Old Testament and the New Testament are linked together and this is amply shown by this passage where Jesus Himself reads Isaiah's words. He confirms that He is the fulfilment and enactment referred to by Isaiah. Jesus states that He is the promised Messiah who Isaiah describes. Sometimes, Jesus is called the Word of God made flesh (incarnate), and He tells this to those who are present and have listened to His reading in the synagogue (the local Jewish place of teaching and worship). Today we are fortunate to have both the Old and New Testaments to read and be guided by, which form the complete Bible as we know it now.

The Bible contains the Word of God and Jesus and the Holy Spirit recorded throughout the ages by those special people chosen by God for this task. The Christian faith, history and heritage are fully documented within the Bible. God speaks to us through this special book, the Bible, and we need to listen to God by reading and understanding His Word in the Bible. The Bible is our basis of learning about God, Jesus, the Holy Spirit and also the Devil and man. In today's reading Jesus proclaimed Himself as the Messiah, the Saviour that the Jews were looking for from God and He used the Old Testament writings to show the confirmation of this to the people. Not all the Jews could believe Jesus. Some let their sinful nature be the stumbling block to having the faith to believe in Him. God knew that Jesus would be rejected by man's sin, but Jesus had come to overcome all sin for man and God had a plan to deal with this. Jesus was free from sin and following His crucifixion and death He had the power to redeem the sin of all mankind, which He used over Satan. Jesus ultimately triumphed over Satan and was resurrected and God's plan had succeeded. In this way, Jesus acts as a bridge over sin between man and God, enabling sin to be overcome once and for all by belief in Jesus the Messiah and Son of God. We are aware of this now through the Gospel and New Testament writings. So, the Old and the New Testament parts of the Bible are important in their own right separately and more importantly together. The Old Testament tells the stories of the great prophets and leaders and events of the Israeli nation and God's guidance and care to the nation and people of His creation. The Gospels of the New Testament tell of Jesus and His story and the further books tell of the spread of the faith and belief in Jesus and the Christian way of life.

Jesus is seen to begin His ministry by speaking to the Jews in the synagogues and was generally well received, but in Nazareth the Jews could barely believe He was a local man, the son of Joseph the carpenter. Although they were amazed with His eloquence, they became angry when He predicted they would ask for miracles to be done there, as He had done elsewhere, and that He would not find honour in His home town. They wanted Jesus to do miracles for them, so they could be persuaded to believe in Him. Jesus though never worked any miracle unless it was with the blessing of God, and certainly never misused his divine miraculous power. When Jesus denied them their request, and called their motives into question, they became so angry, they tried to throw Him of a nearby cliff but they couldn't manage it . He left unharmed and went on with His ministry, which He widened to include all people, both Jews and Gentiles. Matthew, (Matt 2 v23), says that the prophecies of the Messiah being from Nazareth are confirmed. For after His birth and escape from Bethlehem (and possible exile into Egypt), Jesus went back to Nazareth with Mary and Joseph. Jesus lived there until He began His ministry after He was baptised by John The Baptist, and now we consider today's reading of Him clearly telling the Jews in His home town that He was the Messiah. It is not certain exactly which prophesy Matthew refers to here, it may be Isaiah 9 v1-7.

Nazareth itself was in Galilee and was an area at that time occupied mainly by Gentiles and was not held in respect by Jews generally. Nazareth was a small place of no distinction, and an unlikely place for a Messiah to have come from. This shows again that God is not concerned with worldly values. Jesus was known there simply as the son of Joseph the carpenter. Jesus grew up among common Jewish people, the people He had come to save. He apparently experienced a normal childhood and early life there, and was all the time preparing Himself for His ministry to begin, and to follow His Father God's instructions. When later Jesus was crucified, Pilate, the Roman governor who ordered the crucifixion, put a notice on the cross, saying "This is Jesus of Nazareth, King of the Jews". That was a further insult aimed at Jesus, and His followers, as if saying, how could a King arise from Nazareth, such an unknown almost unheard of place? Certainly Pilate also, would have regarded Nazareth as an insignificant place, as it was such a small place, of no particular importance to the Roman Empire.

There are many references to a promised Messiah to be sent by God in the Old Testament, and we have already seen some examples in week one's readings. We shall study more in this week's readings and during following weeks. As Jesus appears to fulfill all the many predictions made about this coming Messiah, this gives further confirmation to believe that He is indeed the Messiah. For many people and especially Christians, the Bible is the most important book in the world and its contents, the Word of God, show us the way God wishes us to live our lives. Bible reading is therefore an essential part of our Christian life. It is important we study the Bible carefully and thoughtfully and ask God's help to do this. We can believe what we read in it, though we must be careful interpreting all parts of it in order that we do not to misinterpret it and God's plan for us. Interpreting prophecy is one difficult area, and there have been many erroneous claims (i.e. the world will end at a particular date).

We need to recognise prophets from false prophets today as much as in biblical times. God helped the people do this in the Old Testament through several of His chosen servants (e.g. Moses, Elijah) and in the New Testament, Jesus Himself (and several others) helped the people do this. We recognise prophets from their acts and attitudes, and likewise we recognise false prophets, by similar means, by their acts and attitudes. If their acts and prophecies are successful, they will have been approved by God. If they have attitudes encouraged by God, such as humility, repentance and forgiveness, we are sure they have been approved by God. In contrast if their acts and prophecies are not successful we know them to not have been approved by God. Also if they do not have godly attitudes, but are instead proud and selfish, we know they have not been approved by God, and are actually false prophets. Jesus tells us to check if people are declaring the Word of God using these tests, and if they are they can be trusted and followed. If they do not satisfy these tests they are not declaring the Word of God and should not be followed or trusted. In this reading today, Jesus confirms the prophecies others made of Him. As God's Son He knew the Word of God fully and He confirmed these prophecies were about Him. Jesus often explained the scriptures to people, notably in this passage, and also on the road to Emmaeus (Luke 24 v 13-35). Many people in the New Testament experienced Jesus' knowledge of scripture, and this is further confirmation that He was the Son of God, of God the Father who directed the writing of these scriptures.

There is much argument over the meaning and detail (including historical accuracy and authenticity) of the Bible between and within both Christians and non Christians. To have belief in its contents we do need to take a step of faith. Although God, Jesus and the Holy Spirit are found in the Bible, their existence cannot ever be proved by human endeavour alone. While the evidence in the Bible and around us seems substantial for the existence of God, Jesus and the Holy Spirit, it requires that freewill act of personal faith to confirm their existence to us as individuals and then to affirm this together collectively. God, Jesus and the Holy Spirit will never be totally understood by man's will alone, and it should be sufficient for man to know as much as God wishes and grants us to know, now and always. God guides man in this, through the Bible and through personal experience. God always has believed in man, but God made man to have freewill and requires man to use that freewill to believe in Him. Freewill means man has a choice, so let us choose wisely, so to believe in God, Jesus and the Holy Spirit rather than belief in either nothing, or in every or any thing else.

Further reading - Isaiah 54 v4-11.

Prayer - Lord, thank You for Your Word in the Bible. Help us to read and understand and be guided by Your Bible. Thank You especially for Jesus, Your Son, in the Bible, in the world and in our lives.

Action -
Notes -

Advent 2 Monday (2/2)
The Prophecy of the coming Messiah Jesus

Ezekiel 37 v24-27 (RSV). *"My servant David shall be King over them; and they shall all have one shepherd. They shall follow my ordinances and be careful to observe my statutes. They shall dwell in the land where your fathers dwelt that I gave to my servant Jacob; they and their children and their children's children shall dwell there forever; and David my servant shall be their Prince forever. I will make a covenant of peace with them; it shall be an everlasting covenant with them and I will bless them and multiply them and will set my sanctuary in the midst of them forever".*

Here the Lord God tells the prophet Ezekiel that He will make an everlasting covenant of peace with His people and shall send them a prince forever. This prince is referred to as David. David was a special leader of the Jews, who followed God's ways as best he could, and during David's reign as king, Israel enjoyed relative peace and prosperity. David honoured God through his life and God blessed him. Before he became king of Israel, David had been a shepherd, and God helped him defeat Goliath (the giant warrior champion) and so prevent Israel being defeated in war with the Philistines. David wrote many of the Psalms of the Old Testament, songs and poetry to the praise of God. Several of the Psalms prophesied of the coming of a Messiah to be sent by God to rule His people (Psalms 22, 110). David though was not completely honourable in all his actions and even he was a sinner. He committed adultery (with Bathsheba) and instead of admitting it, and declaring it to Bathsheba's husband, Uriah, David sent him to his death in a futile battle, to try to cover up his sin. David did later repent and ask God's forgiveness, and resumed his honouring of God. David made sure all Israel honoured God and he became a remembered, popular and respected king of the Jews. Most importantly God told David his descendants too would be blessed and that his kingdom would last forever (cf. 2 Sam 7 v16-17). This became well known throughout Israel, and many prophets proclaimed the Messiah would be a descendant of David.

At this time of Ezekiel's prophecy, the Israelites had been in exile in Babylonia and Jerusalem destroyed because they did not listen to God who brought His judgement against them. Ezekiel tells the people that God will restore them and they will return from exile and look to the future golden age with God. Throughout the Old Testament this scenario is repeated, with God's people straying from His commands and God bringing His judgement on them and eventually restoring them. Repeatedly the people have to learn the lesson about God the hard way through judgement of them.

We can link this passage to the New Testament where we can trace Jesus' lineage back through both Joseph, His earthly father and Mary, His earthly mother, to His ancestors and so we find that Jesus' earthly ancestry is from the tribe of Judah, from which David was descended. This line was special, coming from Adam, to Abraham to David. It was the line from which the Messiah was prophesied and expected to come from (Gen. 49 v10). This is discussed and referred to later on other Advent day readings and is referred to by Isaiah. Although this lineage was and still is considered special by the Jews, as the royal kingly lineage, it can be argued that many of the people included in it had serious flaws of character. We have already said that David himself sinned against God and asked for repentance. The lineage includes Rehab who was a prostitute, and Adam and Abraham also sinned, but all asked for and received God's forgiveness and blessing. This again is a paradox, that the people God uses for good, have been sinners themselves. It is often ironic that God calls those who have sinned to become great servants to Him (e.g. Moses and Paul). Thankfully though it is not a prerequisite to be a great servant for God, to have had a sinful former life. There have been many good people become great servants of God. These include people from Old Testament times (e.g. Noah), people in the New Testament Advent story (e.g. Mary and Joseph) and many people through the ages since (e.g. Mother Teresa). God can and does use anyone to do His will (which can include the good, the bad and the ugly!). No human is, or has ever been perfect, except for Jesus who is special and different, as He is also the Son of God.

David's emblem today is a distinctive six-pointed star (hexagram, or Magen David, adopted as a Jewish device in 1873 by the American Jewish Publication Society and now used as the symbol of Judaism). In both Greek and Hebrew the letter D is shaped as a triangle, thus it is thought the star is made up of two D's for the first and last letters of the name David. It is a very old symbol, but in the middle ages Jews were made to wear this to identify them and later in modern times in Nazi Germany the persecuted Jews were again made to wear it. To the Jews it is though, a symbol of honour not of shame. It is now used on the flag of the modern Jewish Israeli nation. For Christians, the representative cross of crucifixion is a constant reminder of Jesus (whether He is shown on or not on it). These two symbols can be combined into a new emblem, with the Cross of Jesus within the Star of David, representing the old and new covenants God has made to all

His chosen people. The expression, Son of David, in the Old Testament often referred to the promised Messiah. However, Jesus Himself though, had to tell the people (Mark 12 v35) that the Messiah was more than only the Son of David, as David calls Him Lord and instructs Him (through the Holy Spirit) to sit at the right hand of God. This clearly would not have been right if He was only the literal Son of David, but shows that David honours the Messiah above himself, and neither claims this title for himself, nor that the Messiah is his literal son.

The expression Son of David refers to the royal lineage from which the Messiah was prophesied to arise. Jesus is, (through his earthly parents, Mary and Joseph), a direct descendent of this royal lineage. Jesus through His heavenly Father, God, has the most royal lineage possible, truly making Him the promised Messiah. Christians firmly believe that Jesus is God's prince, a new David who was sent to establish this covenant for all men. David was a prince of the Jewish nation who became king of the Jewish nation of Israel, and Jesus was likewise through Mary and Joseph by a distant heritage a royal prince entitled to a royal kingship, but His is a universal kingship and kingdom of all nations. The Messiah was to be a very special leader and Jesus is definitely that, God's Son made man. He fulfilled His painful preordained duty to overcome the sin of man finally, by dying on the cross and being resurrected from the tomb. This means that Christians can now meet God as the barrier of sin has been bridged and overcome. While we live, we can be in good relation with God, and in believing in Jesus we can inherit eternal life and so we will meet and be closer to God when we die. We also have been told that Jesus will come again to the earth some time to establish God's kingdom here (as it says in Ezekiel's text). This is a great thing to look forward to ultimately being with God and Jesus and the Holy Spirit.

Here we read the Israelites long to have a special leader again and Ezekiel tells them God has promised them an eternal leader, a Messiah, who Christians now believe and acknowledge to be, Jesus. Jesus is the new David, coming not only for the Jews and Israel, but for all mankind. David proved himself to be courageous and committed to God. Jesus, who was also distantly related to David, also proved this and remained free of sin. Jesus also proved that as the Messiah, He ruled with and through the power of God's love, not with worldly power.

As we go through Advent preparing to celebrate Jesus' birthday on Christmas Day, we look forward to the day when all people will join this celebration. When that happens, God's kingdom will be with us on earth. This was hoped for long ago in Ezekiel's day, and we thank God for those people through history, who point the nations to God, Jesus and the Holy Spirit. One day all nations will be united in God, Jesus and the Holy Spirit, and Jesus' birthday will be celebrated by all.

Further reading - Revelation 22 v1-7.

Prayer - Lord God, we thank You for all the blessings You give us. Help us to serve and honour and praise You and fulfill Your will for us.

Action -

Notes -

Advent 2 Tuesday (2/3)
The Prophecy of the coming Messiah Jesus

<u>Malachi 3 v1 (RSV).</u> *"Behold, I send my messenger to prepare the way before me, and the Lord whom you seek will suddenly come to his temple; the messenger of the covenant in whom you delight, behold, he is coming says the Lord of hosts. But who can endure the day of his coming, and who can stand when he appears?"*

It is thought this reading refers to the coming of the last great biblical prophet John the Baptist who came to prepare the way for Jesus the Messiah. We have already briefly discussed John the Baptist ministry in the readings in Advent week one. Later in Advent week three, we shall more fully discuss the ministry of John the Baptist. In this prophecy of Malachi (the last book of the Old Testament) we have yet another link connection to the coming of the works described by the New Testament. Malachi was prophesying the new age to come and so now we wait for the final new age to come, the establishment of God's kingdom on earth. As we have already said we do not know how or when it will occur but we must always be ready for it as it may happen at any moment.

The book of Malachi is sometimes described as a short summary of the Old Testament; very appropriate for the last book of that section of the Bible. It tells of God's love for His chosen people and reminds them of their sins but restates that God will keep His promise to His people. Today's reading describes the messenger who will come to reconcile the people to one another, and most importantly to God. Then God will not be angry with His chosen people. Again it is stated that the day the prophet comes will be a day of judgement and only those who have obeyed God will find His favour. Sinners will be set aside in no uncertain manner. So we need to look at ourselves and make sure we are doing and obeying God's will and commands if we wish to join in with God in His eternal kingdom. We cannot say we do God's will and not let our actions show that to be true. The prophet will see how the people are, not simply by what they say, but by their actions as well as their words. The book of Malachi finishes with a reference to Elijah (Mal 4 v5-6), the final message is that Elijah will come again before the Lord and Messiah comes. Jesus said Elijah did come before Him, but the people did not recognise him as Elijah, and killed him (Mat 17 v12, Mark 9 v12-13). Jesus was referring to John the Baptist and so this confirms John was the messenger sent before Jesus the Messiah. Only those who speak and act according to God can be sure to withstand the prophet's judgement sent from God.

Elijah, the renowned Jewish prophet, lived during the reign of King Ahab and Queen Jezebel at the time the Israeli nation was divided into two kingdoms, (Israel the northern, and Judah the southern kingdoms). Ahab, was king of the northern kingdom, Israel. He turned from God and encouraged by his wife Jezebel, practised the worship of pagan gods, both Baal and Asherah. These times are described in the books of Kings in the Old Testament. Elijah, the prophet, was faithful to God and called the king and queen to give up these idolatrous religions and return to worship God. Elijah faced many hardships doing God's will, but he succeeded in removing the priests and prophets of Baal and Asherah and turning king Ahab back to worshipping God. Jezebel, who was a wicked queen, never turned to God and suffered an ignominious nasty death (her daughter was Athaliah, who was also wicked and had tried to eliminate the Davidic heritage). Elijah then is one of Israel's greatest prophets, well known by Jews (among the company of Moses and Isaiah). When the angel Gabriel told Elizabeth and Zechariah of the birth to come of their son John the Baptist (Luke 1 v17) he compares him to the prophet Elijah. John the Baptist then was not Elijah himself returned from heaven, but a similar sort of prophet of God, as Elijah, come to call people to God and be the catalyst to start the ministry of Jesus the Messiah. Both Elijah and John the Baptist saw how the Jews had turned from God and they were both called by God to bring the people back to God. The people that did not speak and do God's will, especially after being told to by these men of God, would suffer the poor consequences of rejecting God. However, those who stand with God, will share in God's kingdom.

This is a glorious prize to strive for, to be with God to receive His love and not to be separated from Him. We are fortunate to see how this has been made possible through Jesus. We know how God suffered during the earthly life of Jesus, most especially through the time of His trial and crucifixion and death. God endured all this, to make it wholly possible for His love to come to all people, through His Son Jesus. Jesus fulfils all the prophecies in the Old Testament proclaiming the coming Messiah and the events of His ministry described in the New Testament shows that He was God incarnate (made man). Faith in Jesus on His own is entirely possible from the New Testament writings alone but in combination with the fulfilment of the Old Testament prophecies concerning Him, it is further confirmed and strengthened.

Further reading - Ephesians 1 v3-10.

Prayer - Lord, we thank You for all those who proclaim Your name, let us play our part by joining with them in praising You. Let our Advent praise and joy please and honour You.

Action -

Notes -

Advent 2 Wednesday (2/4)
The Prophecy of the coming Messiah Jesus

<u>Micah 5 v2 (RSV).</u> *But you, O Bethlehem who are little to be among the clans of Judah, from you shall come forth for me one who is to be ruler in Israel, whose origin is from old from ancient days.*

Micah here prophesies that Bethlehem will be the birthplace of a ruler in Israel. This ruler has been expected for a long time and is not just any ruler, but this is a reference to the promised Messiah. In fact Bethlehem was the birthplace of both David and Jesus. Bethlehem has a very long history. There was a settlement there when Abraham travelled from Ur in Mesopotamia to Canaan, which God promised to be the land of his descendants. The knowledge of the early origin of Bethlehem is a historical fact confirmed by archaeological evidence. One of the first mentions in the Bible for Bethlehem was when Benjamin was born near there and there his mother Rachel died after giving birth to him and she is buried there close to Bethlehem (Gen. 35 v16-20). Benjamin was one of the sons of Jacob, who eventually settled in Egypt with his other brothers, who then formed the twelve tribes of Israel. Later Moses led the Israelites out of their slavery in Egypt back into the promised land of Canaan, and the land was divided into tribal areas. After this, Bethlehem is also mentioned in the book of Ruth in the Old Testament. From the book of Ruth, (Ruth 1 v1-22), we read that Elimelech and his wife Naomi and their two sons lived in Bethlehem, but left it because of famine there, to go to live in Moab, a neighbouring but foreign country. Their sons married there in Moab, to Moabite women, Orpah and Ruth, but Elimelech died and ten years later, both the sons died. Naomi was now a widow and she wanted to go back home. Ruth, one of her Moabite daughters-in-law, remained faithful to her, and went back with her to Bethlehem. There, Ruth married Boaz and through this marriage Ruth became the great grandmother of David, and so became a part of the royal lineage the Messiah was prophesied to come from.

Bethlehem was a small town located about five miles south (west) of Jerusalem, and is still there today. It is in the hill country of Judea, at a higher elevation above sea level than Jerusalem. It is often referred to as Bethlehem Ephrathah, but was also called Bethlehem Judah, see 1 Sam 17 v12. Though it was David's birthplace, it was not the place he chose to make the capital of Israel, instead David chose Jerusalem, after he captured the fortress there from the Jebusites. Sometime later David brought the Ark of the Covenant to Jerusalem and later the Temple was built in Jerusalem. David was guided by God in both these actions. Luke, 2 v11, describes Bethlehem as David's town, which refers to it being David's birthplace. Though David's descendants were blessed by God, they could not prevent Israel splitting into two kingdoms. They were unable to unite the Jews in the way King David had done. The northern kingdom comprised ten tribes and was commonly called Israel. The southern kingdom, ruled by the descendants of David, comprised of the tribes of Judah and Benjamin, but was commonly called Judah and included the town of Bethlehem. The northern kingdom Israel, was conquered and wiped out by the Assyrians in 722 BC (it's capital was Samaria). The southern kingdom Judah, had Jerusalem as its capital and struggled on independently, before its fall to the Babylonians in 586 BC. After this, the Jews were taken into exile to Babylon. Both Isaiah and Micah prophesied about the ruin and judgement to come for Judah. Isaiah and Micah prophesied that God's judgement would eventually fall on Judah because of its unrighteous ways, but here Micah prophesies about a final hope for the Jews to come. Micah is encouraging the Jews, saying that while things are very bleak, all is not lost, as there is a great hope to come. Micah says this hope would arise from Bethlehem, and of course this is the hope for the Messiah who would be a leader similar to David, able to reunite and restore the nation. Christians now believe this Messiah to be Jesus, who came to reunite and restore all people to God.

Bethlehem in Hebrew means house of bread, which is appropriate for Jesus who called Himself the bread of eternal life. In Arabic, Bethlehem means house of meat, referring presumably to the many sheep the area supported, as it was also surrounded by sheep pasture land and sheep were bred here and the lambs were offered as sacrifices in the Temple in Jerusalem. This again is somewhat symbolic in relation to the birthplace of Jesus, who also called Himself the good shepherd and also the perfect sacrificial Lamb of God. Of course, Jesus' birth was announced by the angels to local shepherds, as they watched their flocks around Bethlehem. Jesus was born to Mary and Joseph in Bethlehem. Micah foretells here of the distinction and renown which is in store for Bethlehem as the birthplace of the promised new Messiah. This story of Mary and Joseph coming to Bethlehem and the birth of the baby Jesus there, is a well-known one and central to the Advent and Christmas stories. Bethlehem, Mary, Joseph and Jesus are all prophesied about in the Old Testament. Joseph (Jesus' earthly father) lived in Nazareth in Galilee in northern Israel and was engaged to marry Mary, who also lived there. In the New Testament we hear how Mary was chosen by God to give birth to Jesus and how she accepted this word of God, given to her by the angel Gabriel. This, as one might imagine, caused some consternation to Joseph who was unsure whether to go on and marry Mary under these circumstances. He was however, also visited by the angel Gabriel, who instructed him to marry Mary, and so he duly did this.

At that time, the Romans, under Caesar Augustus were carrying out a census of the Roman Empire, which of course included the land of Judea. The Israelites had by tradition been accounted for tribe by tribe, and this was the way this census was to be recorded. Joseph had to take part in this, by registering himself and his family in this census at his ancestral hometown. Luke says that Bethlehem was the hometown of Joseph, presumably meaning where he was born. Bethlehem was the place to register for all people from the House, or family of David, the place where David had been born. We have traced David's ancestry back to Boaz who had been born in Bethlehem and had married Ruth there. This was the ancestral line of Judah, to which the Messiah had been prophesied to arise from (Gen. 49 v10). Joseph was descended from this line, and had probably been born in Bethlehem and so for this census, he had to journey with his family from Nazareth to Bethlehem, to be registered there. This was quite a long journey in those days, around eighty to ninety miles, especially as Mary was pregnant and nearly ready to give birth. Still they both completed the journey and arrived in Bethlehem in time to be registered on the census. This will be discussed again in further detail, during the readings here for Advent week four. So this meant Jesus, the Messiah, was born in Bethlehem as foretold by Micah.

Bethlehem, as mentioned earlier, was close to Jerusalem where the Palace of Herod the Great was, the then ruler and king of the Jews. Herod reigned as a client king under the overall authority of Rome. Herod was aware that a great ruler was foretold to arise from his kingdom but amazingly he did not realise the Messiah would be born in Bethlehem or to whom, or when or how this would happen. He only became alerted to this when the Wise Men visited Jerusalem, looking for the Messiah. This was fortunate, as after the census was complete and the birth of Jesus had happened, both Mary and Joseph took Jesus and left Bethlehem to escape the wrath of King Herod. For Herod had been angered because the Wise Men had not returned to tell him that the Messiah had been born in Bethlehem and where Herod could find Him. So, Herod instructed that all the male babies and young male children under two years old should be killed, in his attempt to destroy this promised Messiah, who he felt was a threat to his own position as King of the Jews.

God did not choose Jesus to be born in privileged circumstances. Jesus the Messiah was born in a humble way, in a humble town and place. Those involved in this birth were also humble before God and man, in contrast to Herod the Great who was a proud and selfish person, and lived in splendour in his Palace in the capital city Jerusalem. Although Herod was a Jew and he restored the Temple, he abused his position and power on many occasions. This was a notable example, murdering the babies of Bethlehem, though it can teach us to use our lives for good, and certainly not to unrighteously hurt and harm others, believing it to be for personal or other benefit. God wants all people and especially those in authority to do good and be humble. Being humble does not mean being weak and God gives all people the strength necessary to achieve His work. Pride can cause many problems. This passage again shows how God uses ordinary people and places to achieve His works, and we see that God's work will be done, despite difficulties. The prophecies that the Messiah would be descended from David and would be born in Bethlehem were fulfilled by the birth there of Jesus.

Further reading - Luke 2 v11.

Prayer - Lord God, we thank You for the world and especially for the Middle East, the birthplace of Your Son Jesus and Promised Land. We pray You will be honoured through the entire world and especially through the land Jesus was born in and lived in, and one day will return to.

Action -

Notes -

Advent 2 Thursday (2/5)
The Prophecy of the coming Messiah Jesus

<u>Isaiah 9 v6 (RSV).</u> *For to us a child is born, to us a son is given; and the government will be upon his shoulder, and his name will be called "Wonderful Counsellor, Mighty God, Everlasting Father, Prince of Peace".*

Isaiah prophesies of Jesus' coming in the future. Jesus is to be born a man, and so is a son, as Isaiah states. Christians believe Jesus not only to be the son of man, but most importantly to be the Son of God. Today's reading is a well known one. The Jewish people all believed that God would give them a Messiah, as prophesied here by Isaiah. Isaiah highlights the regions of Zebulun and Napthali, which were the first areas of Israel conquered by the Assyrians. He emphasises that they will be the first areas to find honour and be set free by this prince of peace. Nazareth, the hometown of Jesus, and Cana are both in these regions and were the first areas to be influenced by Jesus. He lived in Nazareth and from there started His ministry, and performed His first recorded miracle at Cana, and so this is seen to fulfil this prophecy.

Today we have the great benefit of knowing that Jesus was born and lived with man on earth. Before His time on earth no one could accurately predict His life but it appears many Jews hoped for a very different character to change their history. They appeared to look for a more worldly approach, a worldly king, rather than the heavenly king the Messiah is. They were expecting the Messiah to be similar to David. Perhaps they hoped for an easy way of life without their faith needing to be faith of the depth that God wants His people to have in Him. They appear not to have fully understood the words of Isaiah. So today many Jews and others do not acknowledge Jesus as their Messiah, and as Christians do, as the Son of God. Some believe Jesus to have been a religious teacher only. Christians though believe the Bible gives testimony to this prophecy that Jesus is the Son of God and Messiah. Of course Christians have their own personal evidence of their own experience of Jesus through their own lives, which confirms their own faith individually. Still today many Jews are hoping for a Messiah to come and save them (as many other religious sects do). Unfortunately, they have ignored the shouts for joy of the watchmen that we encountered in Advent week one. This is very ironic as Jesus came as a Jew, but has been rejected by some of the very people He came to help. Mary and Joseph did not doubt Jesus to be God's Son and their Messiah, but many of the leading Jewish priests (notably Caiaphas) rejected Him. These priests felt threatened by Jesus, and remained hardened to Him. This had been predicted would happen by many, including John the Baptist and Jesus Himself.

Christians believe that biblical scripture has been fulfilled with the coming of Jesus as the Messiah. The Messiah has lived on earth, He was born in the manger, and He died on the cross and has taken the sins from all people. Now we Christians await His Second Coming, when the full kingdom of God will be established here on earth as well as in heaven. Presently here on earth we have the Holy Spirit to help us. We can also experience God the Son, Jesus, in our lives and spirits, by believing in Jesus. God the Father and God the Son are presently in heaven, and it is God the Holy Spirit who is here with us now on earth. We can of course not only have Jesus in our hearts and souls here and now, but we can have God the Father and God the Holy Spirit within us too. So we can have a kind of heaven on earth, one that is in our hearts. Christians believe when we die we can get to heaven, where we will be with God the Father, God the Son and God the Holy Spirit fully. The Messiah's second coming may happen now or after we have died, but by belief in Jesus we can share in that second coming, the second Advent, whenever it takes place. Few men have experienced God directly (Moses in the burning bush, Isaiah in his vision, Elijah in the still small wind). All people can be certain of one thing in this life, that this life will be the death of them. Christians are though certain of something else, which is that Jesus will be the life of them, now and eternally.

This passage is also well known in Handel's choral work entitled The Messiah. This is a great choral work of Christian celebration. As well as celebrating God in music and song, we can celebrate God in every area of our life, in work and play. In fact there is no area of life that we cannot praise God in. We know that musical celebration was important to the Jews, and they had musicians and singers with specially written pieces to praise God with. Poetry and arts are represented and the Psalms are good examples of this. Many famous people through modern history have been Christians and modern civilization has been greatly influenced by Christians worldwide. Many of these have contributed positively to life in science, health, art and all walks of life, and many of these people have testified how their belief in God, Jesus and the Holy Spirit has helped them in their work and lives.

In contrast, there also have been (and still are), several non Christian and atheist cultures. Some movements have been characterized by religious intolerance and atrocities, especially the Nazi regime which was responsible for persecution of the Jews and the awful Holocaust. Other cultures have instigated racial as well as religious intolerance and injustice (Ku Klux clan, Apartheid etc). Even the Christian church at certain times in differing countries has not obeyed God in some matters, which have occasionally caused pain and injustice. Still today in several countries Christian worship is forbidden and punishable with imprisonment or worse. Jesus emphasises tolerance and love to all people and He and His creed is the one the world needs to follow for fulfilment. Jesus told us His summarised creed, which is firstly to love God and then to love your neighbour as you love yourself. The world has tried many other creeds, for example communism and capitalism but these have been found to be unsatisfactory. Anglican Christians often use the Nicene Creed as their summary of their belief, and recite it in church services. Jesus' creed is, shorter, and simpler and is a super summary to know and follow. Jesus' love covers the whole world and all people and He is our everlasting counsellor, father, and peacemaker. His coming was predicted and wanted by Isaiah, and we thank God for that.

Further reading - Matthew 25 v1-13.

Prayer - Lord, we thank You that Jesus is Your obedient faithful Son, and our Messiah and saviour. Help us and all people, to follow Jesus and to be like Him.

Action -

Notes -

Advent 2 Friday (2/6)
The Prophecy of the coming Messiah Jesus

Isaiah 11 v1-3 (RSV). *There shall come forth a shoot from the stump of Jesse, and a branch will grow out of his roots. And the spirit of the Lord shall rest upon him, the spirit of wisdom and understanding the spirit of council and might the spirit of knowledge and the fear of the Lord.*

In today's reading, Isaiah again confirms that the Messiah will come and will be a descendant of the root of Jesse, the father of David (which was mentioned earlier in Ezekiel's reading). Jesse is directly descended from Abraham, and Joseph, the earthly father of Jesus, is descended from Jesse. God has chosen someone to come from a respected lineage to be His representative, our Messiah. This lineage comes directly from Adam, the man God first made to found the human race. From this direct line came many men whom God favoured and made the basis of the Jewish nation. King David was Jesse's son and God blessed him and promised the Messiah would be one of his descendants. It is also worth noting here that Mary too was a descendant of David. It was important that Joseph was descended from David as this meant he had to go with his family, his pregnant wife Mary, to Bethlehem to register in the census, which as we read earlier brought about the fulfilment of the prophecy that the Messiah would be born in Bethlehem. However, Joseph and Mary's genealogies differ. Mary's genealogy is recorded in Luke 3 v28-38, while Joseph's is recorded in Matthew 1 v1-17. In these genealogical records it is shown that Joseph was a descendant of Solomon, through Jechoniah, whom God had cursed by denying Jeconiah's children the right to lead Israel nor the right to become Messiah. Mary though was a descendent of Nathan, with therefore a legitimate legal claim for her offspring to the throne of David and so also to be Messiah. Isaiah then continues from here to describe that this new king will establish a new kingdom. This will be God's kingdom and this new king will be the ruler. The new king and His kingdom will honour God fully and the kingdom will be a wonderful place, the people will be righteous and there will be no evil in it. This was a wonderful state to hope for at that time and also remains so now.

At this Advent time we are considering and looking to the coming of the Messiah (the anointed one of God). As Christians we believe Jesus is this Messiah and new king. God sent Jesus to His favoured chosen people, the Jews, and through the lineage God had promised to honour from Adam to Abraham and beyond. However what is also important is that although Jesus was born as a Jew to a Jewish family through this favoured lineage, He was sent to be the saviour of all men from all nations. The Jewish nation had had several rejections of God and although originally God's chosen people, God, who has always given His unconditional love to all people, has decided that anyone who believes in His Son will be saved and can come to Him. No one needs to follow the Jewish culture or become a Jew before believing in Jesus.

Isaiah's description of the Messiah is a good summary of the qualities of Jesus. These are qualities of a loving son honouring a loving father. We know that God was with Jesus, through His whole life, and that Jesus was fully obedient to God. Only because of this was Jesus able to overcome sin, the Devil, and death and so rise again immortal and then return home to heaven and to His Father God, this work accomplished. So while we consider the first Advent story and the first part of the Messiah Jesus' mission, we should also look to and remember that His second coming will bring this wonderful kingdom to all people on earth. If Jesus had not been strong enough to follow God's plan, enduring the unjust suffering of crucifixion and battle with sin and the Devil, He would have been overcome by the Devil, and the path for all back to God through Jesus never established. Jesus is the perfect and only example of a perfect person and so is unique in that respect. He never sinned although He was repeatedly sinned against. In this respect He was greater than Adam, the man God made in His own image, and greater than any other man since, including David. Although we can and must try to be like Jesus, we will never get near to His perfection. Jesus is unique as God's Son, not Adam's son (who, in effect, we are).

We thank God for the first Advent that brought Jesus the Messiah as a little known baby, and as Christians we believe in and look forward to the second Advent, preparing for the return of Jesus the Messiah as a well known king.

Further reading - John 20 v29.

Prayer - Lord God, we thank You that Jesus Your Son came to save all men. Help us through this Advent time to get ready for His coming, getting ready to welcome Him and honour Him as Your Son, our saviour.

Action -
Notes -

Advent 2 Saturday (2/7)
The Prophecy of the coming Messiah Jesus

<u>Isaiah 53 v12 (RSV).</u> *Therefore I will divide him a portion with the great, and he shall divide the spoil with the strong; because he poured out his soul to death, and was numbered with the transgressors; yet he bore the sin of many, and made intercession for the transgressors.*

Isaiah foretells Jesus' role in giving His life for mankind with God raising Him high in exultation. This is again another reference from Isaiah to the Messiah Jesus and the role He was to play. This quote refers to the end of Jesus' life and the fulfilment of it. Jesus made the greatest sacrifice of all. As a unique part of God He was sinless and blameless and He broke the hold of death and Satan over mankind by His ultimate self-sacrifice. He went down to death, but Satan did not have the power to take His sinless life and He struggled with Satan but He overcame Satan. Through that time and that self-sacrifice Jesus paid the price for the sins of mankind (especially the sin of Adam and Eve). He had been obedient to God through His whole earthly life and He died for us to fulfill God's plan and will.

Jesus had known joy and suffering through His life, but God had always looked after Him, with the help of loving parents, from infancy, and later even the love of His disciple friends. He had though to endure dying a cruel death and struggling with the Devil, which must have been unimaginable suffering. God's love and power brought Him through and He triumphed, was resurrected and later ascended to heaven, having completed His mission. It is no wonder God honoured Him and in this passage we are told God and Christ also honour all the strong. Who are they? Simply they are any who are like Jesus. Those who are obedient to God and who have faced hardship and suffering for God, but who have followed God's will. We have to thank God that not many of us are called to face the extreme suffering that Jesus did of giving one's own life to save another's life. More importantly we must thank God for Jesus, as we are getting ready for His coming at this Advent time. Often we feel daunted thinking of the strength that we need to do God's will. However, any strength we have (mental, physical and spiritual) comes from God. We can be comforted to know that if we believe fully in God, He will turn our weakness into strength. Simply we cannot do God's will on our own, in our own strength, but we can do it with His help, as God can give us the strength to do His will. We can see many examples in the Bible and further in history where God has chosen unlikely, seemingly weak people to do difficult demanding tasks requiring physical, mental and spiritual strength and God has helped them complete their tasks. God will honour us for any suffering on His behalf and most importantly we can be fully confident that we can now come to God through belief in and love of His Son Jesus.

We are nearly half way through Advent now and have encountered the hope of and prophecy of the coming Messiah from the Old Testament. We thank God for this opportunity to get to know about the Messiah. Hopefully we know the need for God in our lives, which is just as relevant today as in Isaiah's day. Also, we hope we have some more understanding of His Son Jesus, the Messiah, and of the role of the Holy Spirit. We mark this Advent time as special by spending our time exploring these issues. We need to listen and talk to God and one another, by reading, thinking and praying, working and acting as God wants us to at this special time of year. Let our plans and celebrations honour God now and always.

Further Reading - 2 Corinthians 12 v10.

Prayer - Lord, we thank You for Your servant Isaiah. We thank You for his faithfulness and his vision and we pray that You will strengthen us to be Your faithful servants too.

Action -

Notes -

Advent Week 3
Main theme: The Forerunner of the coming Messiah Jesus
ADVENT SUNDAY 3

Luke 3 v2 (RSV). *The Word of God came to John the Son of Zechariah in the wilderness: and he went in to all the region about the Jordan, preaching a baptism of repentance for the forgiveness of sins.*

We have earlier mentioned the prophecies from Isaiah and Malachi that a great prophet would prepare the way of the Lord. We now know this prophet to be John the Baptist the son of Zechariah and Elizabeth (cousin of Mary, mother of Jesus). John the Baptist is the forerunner of the Messiah Jesus, and we shall look at the importance of this during this third week of Advent. John the Baptist's ministry was a baptism of repentance with water for the forgiveness of sins. He had a great impact on the people of his day. Many people came to him for baptism and they recognised the power of God within him. He preached that God would forgive their sins if they would believe in God and repent of their sins. This repentance meant acknowledging that they had sinned, and asking God to forgive their sin, and also pledging to renounce and give up their previous sinful lives and try to come to God to try to lead righteous lives in the future. This is a big life changing commitment. Baptism was meant to be a symbolic cleansing and washing away of sins. John performed this by total immersion in the River Jordan. For many people this act may have required a lot of courage and would certainly be a memorable event. Courage was needed to come to the decision to want to wash away sin, to start a fresh life with God. Courage would also be needed to perform this dramatic baptism publicly. John's work, his ministry of baptism, became well known throughout Israel.

The Jewish nation had become a nation under Roman occupation and the Jews wanted their independence and restoration of their nation. Many Jews were hoping for the Messiah to come and achieve this restoration. John was reviving this hope, though his message was that individuals and then the nation had to turn back to God before restoration was possible. People did listen to John and many accepted his teaching and turned to God through this repentance and baptism. John's message and ministry was for all Jews, though proved most popular with the common people. This is not surprising, as those who had wealth and power had often achieved it through unjust means, and John called for all to give up their unjust lifestyles and honour God by living righteous godly lives. John had little respect for some of the Pharisees and Sadducees, who he called hypocrites because they made a show of believing in God, but were not sincere in their application of belief. John was calling the nation back to God in the style of well known prophets of old, and the Jews started to remember their ancestral heritage. This was the change in the national Jewish religious climate that was to encourage the Messiah to come and reveal Himself. At this time Jesus had not yet started His ministry, but now He recognised this was the right time to start His work. Now though, Jesus also sought John out, and was baptised by John. This was the most dramatic baptism John performed, as at the time the Holy Spirit descended from heaven to confirm Jesus's baptism. This event made Jesus finally ready to begin His ministry and thus John the Baptist's ministry started the ministry of Jesus.

The events of Jesus' ministry were to irrevocably change the world and to fulfil Jesus' destiny and God's promise to save man from sin. John the Baptist was the supreme evangelist whose efforts prepared the right conditions for Jesus's ministry to begin. John preached the good news about God, and telling people to renounce and turn from their sin to God. John the Baptist was a great man of God with a special mission, to prepare the right conditions for Jesus to start His ministry. John was the catalyst that started Jesus on His ministry of the good news of God. For Jesus, this ultimately was to lead to His death by crucifixion and then His resurrection leading to salvation for all mankind. So as we prepare for Jesus's birthday we should give some thought to being evangelists ourselves, and try to emulate the strength and obedience that John was blessed with and demonstrated. John's life and ministry was largely centered in the desert wilderness. He went to a place free from other worldly distractions, to somewhere where God's presence could be simply encountered and acted on. Are we able to find a similar place to be with and honour God in? There are many wildernesses and deserts in the world, areas of tough and harsh conditions and practically devoid of life. These are not necessarily natural places, many are man made and some exist in people's hearts and minds. Paradoxically God can be found in, and enter in to those areas, as well as in fine temples and churches. There are parallels between John and Jesus, as Jesus came to the wilderness also, and was ultimately tested there by Satan. John was born about six months before Jesus, and died by the brutal execution of beheading about six months before Jesus was brutally executed by crucifixion.
Many people came to John to hear his message of how to find God, by repentance of sin and pledging themselves to God through the act of baptism, and to follow God's commands in life. There are many

people today searching for fulfilment in their lives. Now by coming to Jesus and having faith in Jesus, they can come to God who is the only one able to provide a fulfilling life for the people He created.
Baptism remains an important act in the Church today. Many Christian Churches perform this and in several ways. It may be with full immersion or by a symbolic partial application of blessed holy water. For Christians it represents declaring your faith publicly before the world, receiving the Holy Spirit, and bringing membership of the Christian Church. Adults, children and even babies can be baptised, although different Christian Churches have different traditions in respect to baptism. There is a world wide Baptist church which is well known, where baptism and the example of John the Baptist is emphasized, and given great importance alongside belief in Jesus, Son of God and Messiah. We thank God for the work of John the Baptist in preparing the way for Jesus to start His ministry. We thank God for all people who have the courage and commitment to be baptised, and for all those who perform these baptisms in God's, Jesus' and the Holy Spirit's names. We also thank God for our Advent preparations, making the way ready for ourselves, and others to experience the coming birth of Jesus.

Further reading - Luke 1 v17.

Prayer - Lord, now we thank You for the life and work of Your servant John the Baptist, who was steadfast in his service to You, and to Your Son Jesus. Help us to play our parts in Your kingdom, now and always.

Action -

Notes -

Advent 3 Monday (3/2)
The Forerunner of the coming Messiah Jesus

John 1 v26 (RSV). *"I baptise with water; but among you stands one whom you do not know even he who comes after me the thong of whose sandal I am not worthy to untie".*

John the Baptist started his ministry believing that the Messiah was in the world and ready at any stage to reveal Himself. John knew his own role was to make the conditions right for the Messiah to appear and begin His ministry. He did not know which one of the many people he was baptising would be the Messiah, but he had faith to know that the Messiah would appear to him and the people. Many people witnessed and recognised John's power, which was that the power of God was within him. John said clearly someone was present who was so much greater than he was, and this may have worried and excited many people.

John clearly knew that he was the forerunner of the coming Messiah. Perhaps some people were confused by John the Baptist and may have cast him in the role of a leader, as they were hoping for a leader to make a better, stronger Israeli nation. In this verse John clearly states that he is not the hoped for leader, the expected Messiah, but that the Messiah will appear after his work is done. The Jews directly asked John who he was, but John replied initially who he wasn't. He said he wasn't the Messiah, nor Elijah, nor the prophet like and promised by Moses, but that he was the one proclaimed by Isaiah, shouting in the desert to make a straight path for the Lord. John however, was clear in his role that he was to preach anew the teaching of repentance to the nation. John baptised all people with water, which was a ceremonial cleaning and washing away of sin. The water can also be thought of as the water through which Moses led the people out from Egypt through the Red Sea. It may also be thought of as the waters of birth, thus signifying a person's new birth. John baptised in the river Jordan, by full immersion. This river runs through Israel from its sources around Mount Hermon in the north into Lake Huleh and on to the Sea of Galilee. From there it descends about sixty-five miles to the Dead Sea further south (the Dead Sea is below sea level and has no outflow). The river Jordan runs through the desert wilderness that John had gone to, in order to be with God, and where the people followed him. The river brought life giving water to the area it traversed and John used it to bring life to the people who came to him there through baptism in it.

Water may also be thought of now as representing Jesus, who likened himself to a stream of living water, giving eternal life (John 7 v37-39). Water is essential for life as without out it we become thirsty and die, and it also represents Jesus being killed and rising to new life. Baptism is meant to remind us of Jesus dying to overcome sin and being resurrected to a new life. This can be compared to being born again, not only in a physical sense but also in a spiritual sense. It is a symbolic birth both into the physical and spiritual family of God, into the Church of God. Water needs to be used responsibly, as if we have too much we become ill and could die (by drowning) and again too little can make people and other living things ill and even die. The water of Baptism is special as it has been blessed by God. In contrast, we cannot have too much of Jesus, though we need to be responsible in our use of the living eternal water of Jesus. Jesus warns us of this, misuse of the name of God, Jesus and the Holy Spirit is an unpardonable sin. Also, we know that many Christians suffer for their belief in Jesus, from those people who do not believe in and actually oppose Jesus and Christianity.

The Jews also asked John why he was baptizing people and in this reply he says the Messiah is already here and will soon be known. John infers by this, that his baptisms are needed before the Messiah reveals Himself, and so he is reinforcing Isaiah's prophecy about himself, that doing this is necessary to prepare for the coming of the Messiah. Shortly after this John says that the Messiah will baptise also, but the Messiah will baptise not with water, but with a greater gift, that of the Holy Spirit.

Further reading - John 7 v37-39.

Prayer - Lord God, we thank You for the act of baptism that brings the gift of Your Spirit to make us be born again of You.

Action -

Notes -

Advent 3 Tuesday (3/3)
The Forerunner of the coming Messiah Jesus

<u>Luke 1 v36 (RSV).</u> *"And behold, your kinswoman Elizabeth in her old age has also conceived a son; and this is the sixth month with her who was called barren. For with God will nothing be impossible".*

The angel Gabriel tells Mary of her role to come, and here tells her that God has allowed Elizabeth (her cousin) to be pregnant with a son. Elizabeth's pregnancy was amazing and the angel used it as another example that God can make seemingly impossible things happen. This pregnancy resulted in the birth of an only son, named John, who later became known as John the Baptist.

John was a miracle from God to his God loving but ageing parents, Elizabeth and Zechariah. They had no children and Elizabeth was thought to be unable to have children (barren). Zechariah, John's father was a priest at the Temple and during his duty there he had a visit from the angel Gabriel. Gabriel told him God was going to give him and Elizabeth a son, who would be the special person foretold by the prophets, to prepare the way for the Messiah. The angel told him to call him John, though Zechariah questioned if this could happen because he and Elizabeth were old. The angel rebuked him for not having faith in God to make this happen and said because of his doubt, he would be made dumb from then until the baby was born. Later when John was born, Zechariah and Elizabeth were asked by their friends and relatives what to call him and Elizabeth said John. When Zechariah was called for his opinion, he wrote the name John on a tablet and everyone was amazed, but this had been what the angel had told Zechariah. Normally a family name would have been used to name the son, but unusually, no relatives had been called John before. At this point, Zechariah became able to speak again and he praised God and told of John's coming ministry. God had marked John out as a special person with a vital duty to perform. John was to be the great man of God who would prepare the way for the Messiah.

All this happened shortly before the birth of Jesus, and we know Mary then goes to see Elizabeth and spent time with her before John was born. When they first meet at this time, Elizabeth recognises that Mary too is pregnant and that Mary and her baby to be, are very special, having also been honoured by God. This must have been a great encouragement to Mary, further strengthening her belief and faith in God. Both women were obedient to God and they knew their sons were specially chosen and blessed by God to do His will. Their children were to be dedicated to God to live to fulfill this special plan of God to bring the Messiah to the world. While they knew this, neither mothers knew how God would actually make this happen, but they trusted in God completely. There is no further reference to Mary and Elizabeth meeting again in the Bible after this. It is probable that while Jesus and John knew of each other's existence, they never met until Jesus came to John in the wilderness to be baptised. In the rest of this week, we hear how John was set apart and led his holy life in the wilderness. We have seen in other references (Matthew 3 v 3) that John was the man of God foretold by Isaiah, who was to prepare the way for Jesus the Messiah. As we are now preparing for the birth of Jesus which leads on to Jesus' life and ministry, we can see how these events were intimately associated with the birth, life and ministry of John the Baptist.

As Mary hears the angel tell her what God had done for Elizabeth, it seems to have helped her accept what God had planned for herself and she replied to the angel she was Gods servant. She did not question her planned role as mother to be of Jesus, and simply told the angel that these events would happen to her as God decreed. The rest of this chapter in Luke tells of the further story of John, and Mary returned home to Nazareth after staying three months (just before the birth of John). John and Jesus were both born to mothers committed to God, in families committed to God. These families loved God and were loved by God. Their love for God was shown by their obedience and service to God, and they remain examples to all men and women to love God through their whole lives.

This Advent we think of the miracles that God worked to bring His Son, our Messiah to us. We can think of the miracles of these extraordinary births, of John and Jesus, and of the miracle of all births. We can think of the miracles of these extraordinary faiths, and of the miracle of all faith. As we do so, we remember, "with God nothing will be impossible". What miracles are around us at this time and what miracles will God work through our faith in Him in our lives?

Further reading - James 5 v7-10.

Prayer - Lord God, nothing good is impossible with You. Thank You for the example of John's parents and Jesus' earthly parents who loved and believed in You, Your Son and Your Holy Spirit.

Action -
Notes -

Advent 3 Wednesday (3/4)
The Forerunner of the coming Messiah Jesus

Matthew 3 v16 (RSV). *And when Jesus was baptised, he went up immediately from the water, and behold, the heavens were opened and he saw the spirit of God descending like a dove, and alighting on him; and lo, a voice from heaven, saying "This is my beloved son, with whom I am well pleased".*

This was the momentous occasion when Jesus was baptised by John the Baptist, and Jesus received the Holy Spirit directly from God. John's purpose has now been achieved, and indeed he prepared the way, as Jesus, the Messiah, is now ready, blessed by man and God and prepared to start His ministry. From this point Jesus went into the wilderness and was later tempted there by the Devil. Jesus then left the wilderness and began His ministry, journeying throughout Israel. Jesus, like John, called the people to God and began to show them that He was the Messiah. John stayed in the wilderness waiting for an opportunity to help when called on by God or Jesus. John experienced this moment and now while he at last knew that this Jesus was indeed very special, to receive such a blessing from God, and likely to be the promised Messiah, he may still not have either fully understood or believed that Jesus was indeed literally the Son of God.

Baptism is a person's spiritual birth. It is a time to repent publicly of your sins and publicly ask God, Jesus and the Holy Spirit to come into your life. It was as necessary for Jesus, the Son of God as it is for every church member today. Except Jesus was free of sin and His baptism did not mark an act of repentance for Him, rather it was an act of honour for Him, asking His Fathers blessing publicly. For everyone else baptism is a public mark of repentance to God and the moment you choose to declare publicly your faith in God and to receive His Holy Spirit. Jesus was though born again of God by His baptism, just as all who are baptised are born again of God. For all people baptism is a special time, and this baptism was an extraordinarily special one. Jesus, God's Son was blessed by God His Father, a very special moment for God. Jesus was anointed by John the Baptist and by this action, directly by God. Messiah means anointed and Jesus was anointed by the highest authority, by God. When Jesus was later presented as a baby to God in the Temple in Jerusalem, there was a special confirmation that He was the promised Messiah, the message from Simeon. Here, though God directly confirms Jesus to be His Son and fully blesses Him with this Holy Spirit. Jesus was baptised by John the Baptist, a special man of God, while others receive the baptism from priests, who are other men specially blessed of God. John had said he should be baptised instead by Jesus, but Jesus knew he had to submit to John's baptism like everyone else had done. This confirmed John's role and importance and led to this miraculous baptism, revealing Jesus' true identity as the Son of God and Messiah. We read earlier that John states when the Messiah comes, he will baptise with the Holy Spirit (Mat 3 v11). Jesus is our high priest to God. Jesus accepted John's blessing and also directly received His Father's blessing as the Holy Spirit and we pray that we receive this as we are baptised also.

This marks a special time for many people, as well as Jesus, especially Mary and Joseph, Elizabeth and Zechariah and also God. These were the earthly and heavenly parents of Jesus and John and we will further study their involvement in the Advent story next week. This baptism was an important point in Jesus' life, as after that, He resisted the Devil in the wilderness and He then began His Messianic ministry. This ministry further confirms to Christians and to all who would believe in Him, that He was the Son and promised Messiah of God, though this is more fully explored in the Church's seasons after Advent.

Further reading - Galatians 4 v4-7.

Prayer - Lord, we thank You for our baptisms and for all people who have been baptised and that we will all remain strong in our faith and honour You eternally.

Action -

Notes -

Advent 3 Thursday (3/5)
The Forerunner of the coming Messiah Jesus

<u>Luke 3 v18 (RSV).</u> *So, with many other exhortations, he preached good news to the people. But Herod the tetrarch, who had been reproved by him, for Herodias, his brother's wife, and for all the evil things that Herod had done, added this to them all, that he shut up John in prison.*

Today Luke tells that John was imprisoned by Herod Antipas, one of the rulers of the Jews. Luke says that John preached good news, that God would forgive sins, if the people repented and were baptised. John though insisted everyone should repent of their sins even and including the rulers of the Jews. Here in particular, John challenged the ruler Herod Antipas (one of the sons of Herod the Great), who was the Tetrach of Galilee (north west Israel) and Peraea (east bank of Jordan). This was the area in which John was baptising, and included Nazareth where Jesus lived. Herod Antipas inherited this territory and authority and seemed to have inherited several of his father's personal characteristics. His father had done much building and rebuilding and Herod Antipas also instigated a building program in his territory. Firstly he improved Sepphoris which was only five or so miles from Nazareth. He also built Tiberias in honour to the Roman Emperor which was on the west shore of the sea of Galilee (renamed the sea of Tiberias). He built a second palace at Livias (Julias) about 6 miles north east of the Dead Sea.

Herod Antipas also appeared to have inherited his fathers' brutal streak and disregard for others. The problem for John was over Herod's recent marriage, and because of John's condemnation of this Herod arrested John, and imprisoned him at the fortress of Macherus, about five miles east of the Dead Sea. Apparently Herod somewhat liked John, but was not willing to renounce his evil practices but John was insistent he do so. Herod had divorced one wife (Phasaelis daughter of Aretas 1V, King of Arabia), to marry Herodias. Herodias had been the wife of his half brother Herod Philip the Elder (sometimes named Philip 1), who lived in Rome, and took little to no part in Judean politics. Herod desired to marry her and she agreed and left Philip, to marry and live with Herod Antipas, and she took her daughter Salome with her. Herodias was also the daughter of another of Herod's half brothers, Aristobulus (he had been put to death by his father Herod the Great). Marriage to a women who was both one's sister in law and one's niece was very unusual. This then was an adulterous sinful relationship according to strict Jewish law. Leviticus, 18 v16 and 20 v21, tells that it was illegal for Jews to have sexual relations with a brother's wife, if the brother was still alive. There existed a different state in Jewish law in regard to the widow of a deceased childless brother (Deut. 25 v5). In that situation the other brother was under an obligation to marry the widow and provide a child descendant (see Mark 12 v19) but this was not the case here. John the Baptist wanted Herod Antipas to denounce his marriage to Herodias. Herod though was unrepentant of this act and because John would not change his criticism of this, Herod imprisoned John.

Herod also seemed to respect and admire the popularity John had with many of the Jews but was also probably fearful of this popularity. John's belief in God was so strong that he had challenged Herod to publicly renounce his wrongdoings and John was prepared to undergo the punishment and suffering that Herod could apply to him, rather than back down on this issue. John was also an enigma to the established Jewish church and earlier in his teaching John had castigated many pious religious sects who had come to him (notably the Pharisees and Saduccees). John himself did not change, even when Herod imprisoned him. John remained true to himself and God under this severe test of imprisonment and punishment. Would we suffer for our belief in God and righteousness? Eventually John was brutally executed, by beheading, on the order of Herod Antipas. Herod was tricked into ordering this execution by his wife, Herodias, when Salome, Herod's daughter in law, had pleased him with a dance and he promised to give her any reward she wanted. She asked her mother Herodias what to ask for, and her mother told her to ask for John the Baptist's head. Herod seemed surprised and troubled by this, but felt he had to do as he had publicly promised for Salome, and he had John beheaded. However he continued to feel troubled and remorseful about this afterwards. Herod Antipas was the ruler and so most powerful person of the Jews in that area of Galilee and Perea (but not of all Israel). He was not king, but was titled a Tetrach, left in this power by the Roman Emperor. He blatantly misused his powers, and showed himself to be above the Jewish church and state laws (he acted in a similar way to his father Herod the Great).

Herod Antipas, was one of the sons of Herod the Great, who until his death shortly after Jesus birth had been king of all the Jews, whose kingdom was roughly the same as that of Israel. When Herod the Great died this kingdom was split into three regions, each ruled by one of three of his sons. The two other sons were Herod Archelaus, and Herod Philip the Younger (sometimes called Philip 11), and Herod Antipas was the third son. Herod Archelaus ruled over the southern territory of Judea, but only till AD 6 when he was exiled and replaced by a Roman governor. Archelaus again had been like his father, and was not popular and it was the Jews that asked the Romans for his removal from office. The other son was Herod Philip 11 (or Philip the Younger), who was Tetrach in the area to the north east of Galilee, and he later married Salome. Jesus earlier when a baby and young child, had reason to be afraid of Herod Antipas' father (Herod the Great), who was king when Jesus was born. Herod the Great had felt threatened by the prophecy of the birth of the Messiah who was to be the new king of the Jews, and Jesus had to lie low to escape his notice, to ensure His own safety. We have already briefly mentioned this and will examine it again after Advent.

Later, after John's death, and after Jesus was arrested by the Jewish church leaders, on unjust charges of blasphemy and civil disturbance, Jesus was delivered to Herod Antipas. Initially, the Jewish high priest had taken Jesus straight to Pilate the Roman Governor, for trial to face the death penalty (by crucifixion). Pilate didn't want to deal with Jesus though and when he learnt Jesus was from Nazareth, an area under the control of Herod Antipas, Pilate sent Him to Herod to deal with Him. Herod was there in Jerusalem, celebrating the feast of the Passover. Herod was pleased to meet Jesus, though proved weak and Jesus had nothing to say to him, knowing his many crimes especially the murder of John. Jesus earlier had referred to Herod as a fox (Luke 13 v31-33). Like John before him, Jesus was critical of Herod, but Jesus' condemnation of Herod at this meeting was through silence. Herod Antipas stubbornly refused to repent, and instead mocked Jesus and sent Him back to Pilate, insisting Jesus be put on trial for civil unrest, wanting Him put to death by the Roman method of crucifixion for criminals. This time Herod wanted Jesus dead, but was possibly scared of doing this himself, maybe after the grief and trouble he personally felt after John the Baptists death. Herod did nothing for Jesus, but gave the Romans the responsibility for putting Jesus to death. Pilate somewhat reluctantly, gave in to Herod Antipas and the other Jewish religious authorities and the angry mob calling for Jesus' death. Pilate seemed to see that Jesus had committed no crime deserving of death, but he was very concerned about the political situation and potential for Jewish civil revolt that was surrounding Jesus, and so Pilate gave the order to have Jesus crucified. Nonetheless this collaboration between Pilate and Herod Antipas seemed to improve the previously strained relations between them.

Meanwhile Herod Antipas' problems continued, as later Aretas1V waged war successfully against him mainly because Herod had treated the daughter of Aretas so poorly in divorcing her to marry Herodias. Herod's army was defeated and a Roman army was sent to help Herod and eventually defeat Aretas to restore order to the Roman empire. Herod Philip 11 died in AD 34, soon after the crucifixion and death of Jesus. Philip 11 had been married to Salome but had no children and therefore no heir to his title and land, which was then incorporated into the Roman province of Syria during the reign of Emperor Tiberius, who had by now succeeded Augustus. Then, when Tiberius died, Caligula became Roman Emperor. Caligula then gave this land, along with the title of king, to Agrippa 1, who was a grandson of Herod the Great (from his father Aristobulus, son of Herod the Great, whom Herod the Great had murdered). Agrippa 1 had spent much time in Rome and had become a friend of Caligula. However, Herodias wanted Herod Antipas, her husband, to have these lands and the royal title (not her brother Agrippa) and persuaded him to appeal to Rome for this. Herod Antipas followed her advice and did this, but was, at the same time, accused of treachery against Rome by Agrippa 1. Antipas was not rewarded with his request, but instead was sent into exile in Gaul by Caligula, the Roman emperor, and his lands passed on to Agrippa 1. Herod Antipas' marriage to the ambitious Herodias had caused much difficulty and many Jews and others thought God brought him to ruin because of this, especially in regard to the killing of John the Baptist. Herod Antipas died in exile and Herodias who had remained with him in exile never accomplished her ambitions.

The Herod dynasty then continued with Agrippa 1 who was later also given the lands of Judea by Emperor Claudius when he succeeded Caligula. Herod Agrippa 1 then again ruled over the whole region of Israel and he persecuted the early Christians, putting James the Apostle to death and had Peter arrested (Acts 12 v1-6). When he died around AD 44, (see Acts 12 v20-25), his son Agrippa11 only inherited the northern part of the kingdom. Herod Agrippa 11 also figures in the New Testament, but only in a small way, compared to Herod the Great and Herod Antipas and Herod Agrippa 1. Along with Festus, the procurator at Caesarea, Agrippa 11, heard Paul speak (see Acts 25 v13-26 v30) in his defence. He agreed that Paul could have been freed, except that Paul had appealed directly to the Emperor, and so was to be sent to Rome, to be judged there by him personally. Finally though with the death of Agrippa 11, the Herodian dynasty ended.

This Herodian dynasty played an important part both in the Advent story and in the early Christian story. Jesus was made an outcast, a refugee, by Herod the Great, and had to avoid him to save and preserve His life. Later, both John the Baptist and Jesus were murdered by the actions of Herod Antipas. Both Jesus and John the Baptist remained faithful and obedient to God in these terrible circumstances, which led to their deaths. Ultimately though this has opened the way to eternal life for all people now, through believing in Jesus, who, by His resurrection has triumphed over sin and death. Let us try to remain faithful to God during good times and during bad times, as both John and Jesus have shown they did. Whatever circumstances we are in personally we need to praise God, especially now at this time, for the coming birth of Jesus our Messiah.

Further reading - Galatians 2 v20.

Prayer - Lord God, we thank You for Your help to us and to all who believe in You. We especially thank You for Your help to those people who are presently suffering, and to all who have previously suffered for Your glory.

Action -

Notes -

Advent 3 Friday (3/6)
The Forerunner of the coming Messiah Jesus

<u>Matthew 11 v2 (NIV).</u> *When John heard in prison what Christ was doing, he sent his disciples to ask him "Are you the one who was to come, or should we expect someone else?".*

It appears here that John has doubts about Jesus and is compelled to send his disciples to ask this question of Jesus. Did he actually have this doubt himself, or was he asking this on behalf of others? We know he was aware that Jesus was special after his experience of baptising Jesus, and he had been convinced then that Jesus was the Son of God. Perhaps John asked this both for himself and for others. It must have been so difficult for John, being in prison at that time and not being able to go and see Jesus and personally ask this himself. We have seen that John had absolute faith and belief in God. His whole life was dedicated to God and he was enduring unjust punishment for doing God's will. Doubt is a test of faith and John here tests his faith, and probably the faith of others, in Jesus being the Messiah.

Lots in the Bible, both Old and New Testament was not spelled out unequivocally and similarly Jesus' answer is not a direct "Yes", but rather an implied "Yes", one that needs faith in God, Jesus and the Holy Spirit for its full affirmation. Jesus actually told them to be aware of His work and actions, and that they should decide for themselves if these were the deeds of the prophesied Messiah. He implied that His identity could be revealed by His deeds, and this is how the Old Testament prophecies would be fulfilled. He had done many notable good deeds, including healing physically and mentally, and much teaching and several miraculous acts. Jesus had no need to tell the people around Him that He was the Christ, the Messiah, when they had clear evidence of His personality and behaviour. It meant little to Jesus to have to tell those around Him directly that He was the Messiah. Instead it meant so much more to Him to have the people around Him believe Him to be the Messiah not because He said that, but because they believed that from His actions. God and Jesus want people to make their own minds up about them, which takes a greater commitment than simply being told. It is by this faith commitment that people come to Jesus and God, by their own freewill. Also, if Jesus had at any time clearly told people He was the Messiah, some would have resisted Him much more, and try to call Him a blasphemer, and this was not part of Jesus and God's plan at that time. Jesus though did face this charge of blasphemy on several occasions, most notably from Caiaphas. Under strict Jewish law this was a crime punishable by death if proven, but under the Roman occupation, the Jews did not have the authority to put people to death, instead this punishment had to be approved by Roman authority. So, Jesus gave this reply to John's disciples, and then He continued to do more healing and ministry, which further reinforced His authority and gave more reason to believe in Him.

It is not recorded what John thought of this when his disciples reported this answer back to him, though it is reasonable to assume this reply satisfied both John's disciples and John himself.
John the Baptist's call to Israel and all men to repent and be baptised was rewarded with the Messiah, Jesus acknowledging this call, being baptised Himself, and starting His Messianic ministry. John wanted God's kingdom to come and he knew if Jesus was the Messiah, then He would bring the Kingdom of God and the judgement of God. John's disciples confirmed to him the actions of Jesus were those of the Messiah, demonstrated by Jesus' works of healing, and the miracles He performed and His ministry to the poor. These actions were so special and different they could only be part of the Kingdom of God and the judgement of God was expected to follow. John probably will have instructed his disciples to be obedient to Jesus as the Messiah. In this way there would be no conflict between those presently helping John and those chosen to help Jesus as disciples and all the people who were starting to believe that Jesus was the Messiah. In fact earlier, two of John's disciples had become disciples of Jesus (John 1 v35-42). This was the day after Jesus' baptism when John the Baptist pointed Jesus out to them, describing Him as the Lamb of God, in other words, the Messiah. One was Andrew, and the other was thought to be the gospel writer John, and both were later chosen by Jesus to be Apostles.

After John was killed by Herod, John's disciples buried his body and went and told Jesus about this (Mat 14 v12-13). Jesus went away to a remote place on his own to consider this, presumably upset and troubled by this and needing to pray to God. Jesus was not given much time by Himself though as crowds of people followed Him and He soon became concerned for their welfare and resumed His work by performing another miracle to feed them all.

Further reading - 1 John 2 v24-28.
Prayer - Lord, we thank You that at times of doubt, You carry us and strengthen us. Let our faith in You grow at all times, so that we will be with You in glory wherever we are. Help us remember and help those

in difficulty and in any sort of trouble at this time of the year and help us to bring the news of the birth of Your Son into their lives.

Action -

Notes -

Advent 3 Saturday (3/7)
The Forerunner of the coming Messiah Jesus

<u>Matthew 17 v12 (NIV).</u> *But I tell you Elijah has already come and they did not recognise him, but have done to him everything they wished. In the same way the Son of Man is going to suffer at their hands.*

In this reading, John's importance as the foretold prophet of the Old Testament who was to come and prepare the way of the Son of God is confirmed and here by Jesus Himself. We have already seen that the Jews asked John the Baptist who he was, and whether he was the expected Elijah. John had stated that he was not Elijah, but he was the foretold prophet of Isaiah, the forerunner of the Messiah. Jesus here though compares John to Elijah, the prophet who the Jews thought would return to announce the coming of God. Jesus tells them that John's significance was not understood and reminds them of the cruel death John suffered and now Jesus tells His disciples that a similar fate awaits Him.

This news generally shocks the disciples. The disciples may have been hoping that Jesus would have brought about a revolution, to bring the Jewish nation back to its former prominence and free it from Roman rule. Although the disciples were Jews they were not fully aware of the prophecies of the Messiah in respect to His death. They did not fully understand the significance that His death was to be. They would have already been shocked at the death of John the Baptist and did not want to contemplate the death of their leader and friend Jesus. They all lived in quite brutal times, where the application of justice was uncertain and often harsh. Also the disciples knew they were part of a religious revolution, that they hoped would build to a crescendo to try effect change in Israel and the world. Jesus was their leader and friend and to contemplate His death was dreadful for them. They thought that act would end the revolution they hoped for, and some of them would be lost without Jesus to support them. So they were scared of this prospect, and also felt if that happened all they had worked for would be for nothing. Jesus knows something of His Father God's plan and that He was to be betrayed and be unjustly condemned and killed. Jesus knew He was the Messiah and that He had to have complete faith in God to face the terrifying challenge ahead of His suffering and brutal death to come. Jesus had faith in His Father God, that if He was obedient to this tough task to come, He would be raised to life and later ascend to heaven, and so return to His Father with His mission as Messiah completed. For now, however,

Jesus only says to them He will die. This was to give them time to consider this fact, and to be aware it would happen.

The baptism of repentance John preached was too hard for some to comply with, notably, Herod (Herod Antipas, son of Herod the Great). John's call to repentance involved renouncing evil and turning to God asking for forgiveness and being washed clean by baptism and committing to do God's will from then on. For some who had power and wealth and were used to sinning, this was too much to do, because they had little faith in God. They felt they would lose their power and wealth and wanted to cling to those worldly ways. They were afraid of God, but not enough to renounce their sin and corruption. Later, Jesus warned that people would find it hard to turn from the qualities shown and pursued by some in the world (lies, greed, envy etc) to the qualities shown by God (love, truth, honesty etc). John the Baptist had died believing that Jesus was the Messiah, bringing the Kingdom of God. The kingdom though did not come to be exactly as John the Baptist imagined, and even John had no idea of the way Jesus the Messiah was to fulfill His role through His death by crucifixion and subsequent resurrection. Today we are blessed that we know this, and now we await the Second Coming of the Messiah with the kingdom of God. We know we can share in this, believing in the blood of Jesus, sacrificed to remove our sins and save us, and all people. Nonetheless, John the Baptist clearly pointed the way to God and the work of bringing man to God begun by him, was continued by Jesus the Messiah. At this Advent time let us work for God in our lives and to bring God, Jesus and the Holy Spirit into the lives of others around us.

Further reading - 1 John 3 v7-10.

Prayer - Lord, You have suffered much for us. We are sorry for all our sins and we humbly ask for your forgiveness. Help us to restore what we have broken especially our relationship with You. Let us and all people come to and be with You now and always.

Action -

Notes -

Advent Week 4 (1/4)
Main theme: The Annunciation of the coming Messiah Jesus (Proclamation to Mary about Jesus's birth)
ADVENT SUNDAY 4

Isaiah 7 v14 (NIV). *Therefore the Lord himself will give you a sign: The Virgin will be with child and will give birth to a son and will call him Immanuel.*

Isaiah foretells here that Jesus will be born from a virgin. This is part of God's extraordinary plan to bring Jesus into the world, both as His Son and also as a Son of Man. From now to Christmas we consider the events of this birth of the promised Messiah. Firstly God chooses the earthly parents for His Son. Jesus' mother is the Virgin Mary. Mary was a devout Jew. We have already mentioned both of the parents of course as they are generally now well known. The chosen father was Joseph, and they were engaged to be married to one another, and they lived in Nazareth in Galilee. However there is not much known about either Mary or Joseph, as there is little written in the New Testament about them, other than being the earthly parents of Jesus. Mary is mentioned in certain other books of the period, notably the Protoevangelium of James, but even these give limited information. It is thought from these accounts that she may have served in the Temple at Jerusalem from around three years old till she was thirteen. It is then thought she may have moved to Nazareth and later became engaged to Joseph.

In the same manner that the angel Gabriel appeared to Zechariah (John the Baptist's father) to announce the miracle of John's birth, he appeared to Mary to announce the greater miracle of the birth of Jesus, God's Son, to Mary. This is known as the Annunciation, the angelic proclamation to Mary about the birth of Jesus. This tells then of the incarnation, that the Messiah, the Son and Word of God was to be made human. Mary was greeted very favourably by the angel, who called her blessed. She was somewhat troubled by the angel's appearance to her, so Gabriel tried to reassure her and then he told her the details of God's plan for her to be the mother of the Messiah.

Here (Luke 1 v26), the angel refers to Jesus's lineage that He is an ancestor of David and will be king eternal, in other words the promised Messiah. We also know and have earlier mentioned that Mary herself was a direct descendant of King David (Mary's genealogy Luke 3 v23-38). Mary takes this announcement in her stride, initially querying that she was a virgin, and as yet has no husband. The angel restates that the child is holy, that He will be named Jesus (Saviour) and also that He will be called the Son of God. Gabriel also says that her relative Elizabeth who was barren (had been thought medically unable to have a baby) was also to have a baby son and that with God nothing is impossible. This announcement helps Mary who takes on this challenge with faith and trust.

Mary then is a wonderful example to all of us to have faith in God, and to do God's will whatever it may be. Mary was concerned she was not yet married, but she put her trust in God to deal with this. The angel afterwards went to Joseph and explained how Mary was pregnant and that Joseph should not break off his engagement to Mary. Mary did not want to be thought of as immoral and impure by being an unmarried mother, and trusted God to sort this difficulty out. Mary may have been chosen to be the mother of Jesus, by God, because as a devout Jew, she believed in God so much. As she was a devout Jew she knew it was a sin in Jewish law to be an unmarried pregnant woman. As prophesied by Isaiah, we are told Mary is a virgin (has had no sexual relations) and it is Mary herself who confirms that. The angel says that the child within her was conceived by God through His Holy Spirit. This reinforces the fact that Jesus would be fully divine and holy of God, and would not be the result of merging of male and female chromosomes, as in human reproduction. Jesus' genes came directly and solely from God alone. This was God's plan, that Jesus should be conceived of Himself and so be divine, but importantly be born as a man, in order that Jesus would know fully the experiences of being both God and man. This is an amazing condition and happened in that amazing way. Jesus was to be the first born son of Mary and Joseph, and the first and only born Son of God. We have seen that it was important for Joseph and also Mary to have their human lineage confirmed as being from the Davidic princely line, making them suitable parents for a future Jewish king and importantly Messiah, of Israel. It was important to establish the divine lineage of Jesus as direct from God, through the Holy Spirit. God chose Mary and Joseph to look after His Son and God trusted them to do this. Mary and Joseph trusted God and both were prepared to do this for God, to be parents to Jesus, to look after Jesus in this special way, as His earthly foster parents.

There were no other witnesses to this angelic encounter and message, but soon after it Mary visited her cousin Elizabeth. Elizabeth praised Mary and discerned she was pregnant and that her baby was most special. Whilst we should be amazed at the marvellous event of the

Annunciation, we do need to plan and prepare for Jesus's birth and not to be paralysed by amazement at this miracle by which God sent His Son to us, from heaven to earth. It is of course an incredible event but one which had been foretold by the Old Testament prophets. We now know that God has kept His promise, of sending His Son our Messiah and Saviour, and all this is fully recorded in the New Testament, and we will see this in the daily readings still to come.

Further reading - Luke 1 v30.

Prayer - Lord God, today we think of and thank You for Mary, the mother of Jesus. She loved You, Jesus and Your Holy Spirit fully. We thank You for her example and pray that we and all people can follow her example in loving You, Jesus and the Holy Spirit.

Action -

Notes -

Advent 4 Monday (4/1)
The Annunciation of the coming Messiah Jesus

<u>Matthew 1 v19- 20 (NIV).</u> *Because Joseph her husband was a righteous man and did not want to expose her to public disgrace, he had a mind to divorce her quietly. But after he had considered this, an angel of the Lord appeared to him in a dream and said,"Joseph son of David do not be afraid to take Mary home as your wife, because what is conceived in her is from the Holy Spirit".*

God develops the story with a further angelic announcement to Joseph. Joseph did not want to marry Mary if he, or others, felt she had had sexual intercourse leading to pregnancy with someone else, as Joseph and Mary were engaged. If they married and a baby was born well before nine months, this would show Mary to have had sexual intercourse before the marriage and this also would have been a scandalous revelation. Joseph did not want anything like this to happen and so considered breaking their engagement and not getting married. Joseph though was also concerned for Mary and did not want to bring her shame and public disgrace because of this. Joseph was contemplating breaking their engagement (betrothal) privately in as quiet a way as possible. Then the angel Gabriel appears and explains to Joseph what has happened to Mary who was his virgin bride to be. Joseph then changes his mind and accepted this fact delivered to him by God's special messenger and took Mary to be his wife. This angelic encounter and announcement reassured Joseph that Mary had not been unfaithful to him and this pregnancy was by divine action, by the Holy Spirit. God had prepared the way for Jesus to be born to a committed couple and had alleviated Mary's earlier worries that she was to give birth as a Virgin with no husband. Joseph is obedient to God and this allows baby Jesus to be born to God loving parents.

There is not much written about Joseph in the Bible. We know of his ancestry, which we have discussed, and will keep referring to, and that angel Gabriel reminded him of, by calling him Son of David. To recap, it is thought he was born in Bethlehem and he was descended from David and so with a claim to the favoured Jewish Messianic lineage. He was apparently living and working in Nazareth in Northern Galilee at the time of this engagement to Mary. We are told he was a just man, and to be called that infers that he was an older man as there was a rank or office of Justus given to those who displayed qualities of justice and responsibility and which was usually held by more experienced mature men. It is not known how old he was but it is thought he may have been a widower before becoming engaged to

Mary. We know that he was a carpenter, but whether he was a cabinetmaker or a house maker is not clear. Was he involved with Herod Antipas' building projects in nearby Sepphoris? Did he supply crucifixion crosses to the Romans? He seems then not to have been a rich man, but he was also not poor, and could support a wife and family. He is last mentioned after taking Jesus with the family to Jerusalem for the Passover when Jesus did not return home with them initially, but stayed in the Temple. Some people feel he may have died sometime between this and Jesus' crucifixion, but this is not certain.

This angelic encounter and message helped Joseph change his mind and not break off the engagement. It allowed him to marry Mary as originally planned and Joseph then to become Jesus' earthly, human father. All life is a gift from God, but this angelic announcement convinced Joseph that this gift of life was an extra special one, enacted by God. Did Joseph know and believe that this baby would indeed be the Son of God? Did Mary tell him this part of the angel Gabriel's message to her? Or did she keep that fact to herself, while affirming that this baby was from God? I believe she would have told Joseph all the story and that he believed her. Did she understand the true meaning the angel implied (that Jesus would really be the divine Son of God) when he repeatedly told her the baby would be called the Son of God, whose kingdom would last forever. This will never be known and is up to our own interpretation and belief. She may have understood that Jesus was to be the fully divine and literal Son of God in all its meanings. Or she may have believed the baby was going to be very holy and was to be called by the title of Son of God by men alone. After all in one way she believed God to be her heavenly spiritual father, so she believed herself and all the Jewish people to be children (sons or daughters) of God in that sense. I believe that she either knew or understood or just simply believed and accepted that Jesus was to be literally and actually the divine Son of God, and that she would be the foster parent as Joseph was also.

The angel gives Joseph an honoured title, Son of David, which reminded him of his kingly ancestry and will have been an encouragement to Joseph. This may be a reason why he was chosen by God for this role. We have earlier discussed the detailed lineage of Joseph and Mary and the similarities and differences in their ancestries. To recap once more, both Joseph and Mary were descended from David, and of the line of Judah, but Joseph was descended through Jeconiah which would not make him eligible to father the Messiah. Mary's line was through Nathan and so she was then eligible to be the earthly mother of the Messiah. This lineage is rather complicated, but of some significance in relation to prophecy of the Messiah. Again like many areas of prophecy it comes down to individual belief and interpretation. On its own it seems to me that it would be difficult for anyone one person to have the exact lineage required by certain Jews to fulfill this Messianic lineage. As it appears noone has absolute proof of their exact lineage, then it is impossible to satisfy or prove this either way. To me, both Mary and Joseph appear to have the correct lineage as far as I can discern from my research, and bear in mind many Jewish records were lost in the destruction of the Temple in AD 70, so it is now impossible to check this further! So, Joseph stands by Mary and goes ahead and marries her and he honours God by becoming the human father to Jesus. Mary and Joseph then played important parts in the Advent story and the subsequent early life of Jesus, and this will be seen in the readings in the Season of Christmas and the Epiphany. We do need to remind ourselves that Jesus was unique in having human parents, who were effectively foster parents, and having God as His direct and Spiritual Father.

We will see that Mary and Joseph take care of baby Jesus, from the moment He was born to the moment Jesus left home in Nazareth to begin His ministry. Parents have the responsibility to bring their children up so they themselves can act responsibly and care for themselves, and Mary and Joseph do this for Jesus. Jesus is to be their son, God's Son, and Son of all mankind. We can take a moment now to thank God for our own parents, and for parents in general. Most parents love their children, but I hope all parents can try to follow the example set by Mary and Joseph, to follow the will of God for their family. We pray for God's blessing on those families that don't follow this pattern, both parents and children. We remember and thank God also for all foster parents and foster families.

Further reading - John 3 v16.

Prayer - Lord, we thank You today for the earthly human parents of Jesus, both for mother Mary and father Joseph. They fulfilled their responsibilities as parents and also as Your servants. Thank You for their example of how we should be as loving parents and as Your servants.

Action -

Notes -

Advent 4 Tuesday (4/2)
The Annunciation of the coming Messiah Jesus

<u>Luke 1 v46 (NIV).</u> *And Mary said: " My soul glorifies the Lord and my Spirit rejoices in God my saviour, for he has been mindful of the humble state of his servant"*

Mary praises the Lord for choosing her to be the mother of Jesus. She has accepted this incredible event and praises the Lord God for His help to her ancestors from Abraham onwards. She acknowledges His care of those who hunger both physically and spiritually and His support of the humble, in contrast to His scattering of those who are proud and rich. She was so willing to live her life for God's praise and glory. Now she was chosen by God, she needed to do so, having the responsibility of giving birth to and bringing up God's Son Jesus. Jesus was to be both human and divine. In respect to His human nature Jesus is sometimes referred to as the second Adam, although while He was made man as the first Adam was, He was also fully divine, which the first Adam was not. Both Adam and Jesus were sons of God in one sense of this, yet only Jesus was the Son of God in both (all) meanings. Jesus would be born of Mary in the same way as all people since Adam and Eve are born by God's will and in this way He would experience human life intimately and fully, but uniquely being the divine Son of God. This is a truly amazing and wonderful state that we can only always marvel at, but be grateful for, as Mary herself was. Again it is a miracle beyond our comprehension, but one that we can rejoice in, again as Mary did.

Mary has become an example to all mothers and all people to follow with her firm belief and trust in God. This and the following verses from Luke have become a famous passage and was developed by the Church into a devotional song of praise (canticle), known as the Magnificat. Mary then stayed with her cousin Elizabeth for three months and then went home to Nazareth. It must have been good for them both to share and support one another during their pregnancies. No doubt they will have prayed to God to be kept safe and healthy and probably to ask what God wanted them to do. Whether Mary was at all fearful of her role as the mother of Jesus is open to speculation. The angel had told her not to be afraid and she must have had a deep faith in God which will have made her courageous and strong and untroubled by the future. Like all mothers to be she will have hoped for a good life to come for her child, but she will have had to learn to share her son fully with God. As Jesus grew up and then left home Mary had to learn to share Him with many people, and Jesus in fact came to be shared by all people. Nonetheless Jesus and Mary developed a special bond, between mother and son and Jesus loved and respected her. Here, Mary shows no fear at all and instead proclaims a glorious tribute of praise to God. All people have a purpose for their lives as part of God's plan for them. Here we see the important roles that Mary and Joseph had been given by God in His plan to bring His Son to the world. Mary had been diligent in honouring God and Joseph was a righteous man (called a just man i.e. a man of justice), and this is a central part of God's plan for every person. God may later call people to do special important work for Him, and this calling can come at any time of life. We have seen God call John the Baptist from the start to the end of his life, and so we see a great variety in God's call to people. Some people that God calls, try to avoid God (Jonah, notably in the Old Testament, ran from God and ended up in a whale, before he realised he should do God's will). Some are called late in life, e.g. Moses. Some unfortunately do not complete God's will (Ananias and Sapphira Acts 5 v1-11) and fall away from God, with their lives unfulfilled. Many that are called by God for His service have previously rejected Him and done wrong, but have changed and finally acknowledged God, repented and ultimately done great things in God's name and for the benefit of others. God though is there for all to come and praise and glorify Him at any time of their lives. Anything anyone does for God, no matter how important or even unimportant is seen and acknowledged by God. In the same way, God sees everything everyone does and things that are wrong (sins) do not credit God or the person doing such things. In the same way parents are saddened and hurt when their children do wrong and especially if this harms others or themselves, God is affected similarly when anyone sins. Jesus led a perfect sinless life and this is the example God has given us to follow. This is the fulfilled life God wants us to have, and by the sacrifice Jesus made for us by taking away our sins, it is an eternal life that is available now to all who will love and follow Jesus.

However, God was pleased with Mary, and honoured her by choosing her to be the earthly mother to Jesus. Let us try to be like Mary and honour, obey and praise God in all areas of our lives, and then like Mary received, we will receive abundant blessing from God. We can praise God in many ways during this Advent time, in our homes, at work, out at play, or in Church, on our own, or preferably in company.

Further reading - 1 John 4 v7.

Prayer - Lord God, we give You thanks for the joy worshipping You brings to You, and to us. Let us rejoice in Your service, as Mary did.

Action -

Notes -

Advent 4 Wednesday (4/3)
The Annunciation of the coming Messiah Jesus

Romans 16 v25-27 (NIV). *Now to him who is able to establish you by my Gospel and the proclamation of Jesus Christ, according to the revelation of the mystery hidden for long ages past, but now revealed and made known through the prophetic writings by the command of the eternal God, so that all nations might believe and obey him- to the only wise God be glory forever through Jesus Christ! Amen.*

Here Paul tells the church at Rome the importance of Jesus and exhorts them to praise Jesus who glorifies God eternally. The imminent birth of Jesus fulfils the prophecies of the coming Messiah but now He is the saviour for all mankind not just for the descendants of Abraham, the Jews. Jesus comes to Jews and Gentiles. This shows God's true love for all mankind which is a wonderful present for all people of the world. God is not just for the Jewish nation but is for all nations and peoples. The Jews had been God's favoured special people but had alternated between obeying God and disobeying God. God does not withhold His love from any person. By believing baby Jesus is God's Son, a part of God's being, anyone can have eternal salvation with God. However we cannot believe only in God the Father alone, if we have heard the gospel message. Through the Gospels and all the books of the New Testament we can now believe in God the Son, Jesus, and God the Holy Spirit. Throughout Advent we see this is a new marvellous message from God that He is coming come into the world as His Son, both human and divine. He has come to us as a person, in a form we can understand. The good news of the gospel stories start with the account of Jesus' miraculous birth, and then go on to tell of His miraculous ministry that ultimately fulfils God's will. Jesus the Messiah is God's ultimate gift to us, sent to give us eternal life.

Paul in his writings does not record and comment about the Advent story and events of Christ's birth. Paul was initially a devout Jew and a non-believer of Jesus as the Messiah. He was instead an active opponent of Jesus and Christians in the early Church. Paul never personally met Jesus, but through his work in persecuting Christians he came to learn about Jesus. He was challenged by God to stop his persecutions and instead become a believer in Jesus. This happened to him in a dramatic way when God directly challenged him while he was travelling to Damascus to continue his work against Christians there (Acts 9 v3-19). He was struck blind and given instruction by God which he obeyed, and his sight was restored three days later and so he became a Christian. He then developed, promoted and promulgated the work of Christians and the early Christian church, having become a firm believer in Jesus.

Although Paul does not mention the Advent story directly this doesn't mean he was unaware of it and of its uniqueness and miraculous nature. Rather, Paul was experiencing the Holy Spirit present after Jesus had ascended to heaven and the effect the Spirit had with the apostles and disciples and all early Christians. Paul by not mentioning Jesus' advent beginnings and birth, is not dismissing them, but he concentrated on and was concerned with the current events that were happening around him and the experiences God brought him. He spent a lot of time and effort explaining the teachings of Jesus, and how Jesus' new teaching meant people should live and behave as Christians. Paul wrote the Acts of the Apostles and several letters to churches in the New Testament, and as a learned Jew was well aware of the scriptures and prophecies. Paul explains the teachings of Jesus, which he states show Jesus to be the Messiah and here at the end of this letter, he confirms and emphasises to the Church that Jesus was the Messiah that the prophets had foretold. We must continue to wait patiently for the day we celebrate His coming, using this time to be well prepared and ready to receive Him. Advent is drawing to an end now, the waiting and preparation time is nearly over. Through the Son, Jesus, we will come to the Father, God, and will receive everlasting and eternal life. To God be the glory forever through Jesus Christ - Amen .

Further readings- Zephaniah 3 v14-18.

Prayer - Lord, thank You for the Christian witness and work of Your servant, the apostle Paul. We thank you that the birth of Jesus is near now and we thank you for our Advent time and preparations. Help us to remain patient and prepared for the coming birth of Your Son Jesus.

Action -

Notes -

Advent 4 Thursday (4/4)
The Annunciation of the coming Messiah Jesus

Luke 2 v1, 3 (NIV). *In those days Caesar Augustus issued a decree that a census should be taken of the entire Roman world. And everyone went to his home town to register.*

This passage from Luke's Gospel, tells why Joseph and Mary went from Nazareth in Galilee where they lived, to Bethlehem the town in Judea because Joseph belonged to the house and line of David. David as we have already discussed was a famous king of Israel who God blessed and God also promised that the Messiah would be descended from David. Joseph's hometown was Bethlehem, which was also the birthplace of David, the earlier great king of Israel, and so because of Joseph's ancestral origin, was where Joseph had to go and take his family to register. Here, Luke says Bethlehem is Joseph's hometown, implying Joseph was born there. We have read earlier how Bethlehem was foretold (in the Old Testament, Micah 5 v2) as being the birthplace of the coming Messiah, and will look at this in tomorrow's reading too. This then was the reason how and why this prophecy became fulfilled. God ensured this prophecy was fulfilled, and it happened through the order of the Roman Emperor, Caesar Augustus, to have this census done of his empire.

Jesus was born at a time of relative peace, when most of the "civilized" known world was under Roman rule, forming the Roman Empire. This was yet another civilization that had taken possession of the promised land of God to the Jews. This census was probably recorded for taxation purposes, although historical dating evidence is unclear. Luke says Quirinius was Governor of Syria at that time, but it appears now to us more likely that around the time of Jesus' birth, Varus was the Governor (4 BC), hence the confusion about this. Some Roman censuses took a long time to complete (e.g. the census of Gaul) and one other explanation could be that a census started in 7 BC by Governor Saturnius may have been completed by Quirinius in AD 6-9. Yet another possible alternative is that it was a census instead for allegiance to Augustus. More debate arises from a document found among the Dead Sea scrolls that detailed the journey of a Jewish woman and her husband going from their place of residence Makhoza to Rabbat in the winter of the first or second century AD. This shows that other people were travelling to record census and property rights and so may support this being the reason Mary and Joseph travelled. Anyway, Luke records it was a Roman census, which resulted in Mary and Joseph going to Bethlehem and that then became the town where

Jesus was born. It is also a possible explanation of why there was no room for them when they arrived, as many other people would have been travelling at the time, to also complete this census. Bethlehem may have been full. After Jesus was born, Joseph may have recorded his family details and Jesus on the census too (again only speculation, with no direct evidence to confirm this).

Other plausible explanations have been put forward instead of the census, as to why Joseph may have gone to Bethlehem at that time. One view is that because of the controversy of the pregnancy of Mary, Joseph took her away from Nazareth for a while, to avoid any embarrassment or difficulty in Nazareth. If that is right, were they going to Bethlehem or did they have to stop there because the birth was so close? A further possibility is that Joseph may have inherited some property in Bethlehem, and if that was so, he would probably have had to register it with the authorities there, and they may have journeyed there to deal with that. Whatever the reason was to travel, this must have been a difficult journey for Joseph and Mary especially as Mary was now close to giving birth. They may have been excited but they were still fully trusting in God to look after them. We are told it was about a three-day journey, but this is not exact and may only mean it took more than two days. We don't know exactly how they travelled. They may have been on their own or gone in a company. Some nativity stories include them with a donkey, that possibly Mary may have ridden on. This may have been correct, but though it would have been possible it is only speculation. They did not know what to expect as parents to be of the Son of God, Jesus, but they were prepared to do God's will and be protected and guided by God. This must have been an extra burden on them to travel at this time, but they had to obey the Roman authority as well as God's authority. They would have known it was likely Mary would give birth while away, but were trusting God to take care of them, no matter what their circumstances were.

Did they realise the significance of Jesus being born in Bethlehem to fulfill the Old Testament prophecies? They may or may not have known this, it is impossible to be sure. God looked after them on their journey here and kept them safe, and we need to trust in God to look after us and keep us safe. Here and elsewhere we see how we must trust God to guide us and guard us on a daily basis. We can and must plan ahead, but we do not need to worry about the future, and need to rely on God's love and protection for us now. Let us keep God at the centre of our daily lives, and involve God in everything we do every day. As we journey through life we need God with us as He will show us the right way to go and the right things to do daily. May God be with us now and during these final days of our Advent journey.

Further reading - Isaiah 56 v6-7.

Prayer - Lord God, we thank You for guiding Mary and Joseph on the journey to the place You chose for Jesus to be born. Let us follow You faithfully to the right places You have chosen for us to go to in our lives.

Action -

Notes -

Advent 4 Friday (4/5)
The Annunciation of the coming Messiah Jesus

<u>Luke 1 v 51-53 (GNB).</u> *He has stretched out his mighty arm and scattered the proud with all their plans. He has brought down mighty kings from their thrones, and lifted up the lowly. He has filled the hungry with good things and sent the rich away with empty hands.*

Mary continues her testament of praise of God to Elizabeth. God is about to come as baby Jesus, and Mary reminds us what wonderful things God has done in the past. Mary is pleased that she has been chosen by God, to be the mother of Jesus. She is pleased that through her God has come to help the Jewish nation, Israel. The love of God will be given to those who honour God, but those who do not will not be blessed. Within baby Jesus lies the power of God, and when He is born and in the crib, we are privileged to know that He will grow into Jesus the man, who endures the cross with the hope of resurrection and redemption to come. Jesus comes both as the Son of God and also as the Son of Man and we have talked about this before as it is so important to remember Jesus the Messiah is the special person who was born not only a human, but also a holy special part of God. To best recognise this we need the qualities of reverence and humility that Mary had and that God loves in people. To believe in the coming of God, as Jesus, we need faith. Mary had faith and belief in God. She had come to this through her journey in life, though she seems to have a childlike trust, belief and faith in God. We have seen through these Advent readings reasons for faith and belief, from the founders of the Jewish nation, in the prophets, in the disciples, the Gospel writers and others. We can believe in Jesus because of these reasons and from our own experiences. We can believe in Jesus for many reasons and in many ways, but it is also simply possible to believe in Jesus in a spirit of childlike trust.

The Advent story continues and Mary left Elizabeth and went home. Meanwhile it was time for Elizabeth to have her baby, and John the Baptist was born. His father Zechariah's sight was restored when he was named John. John was dedicated to a special life of service to God. John and Jesus appear never to have met until John baptized Jesus, when Jesus was about thirty years old. They would have known of each other, but it is not known what Mary would have told Jesus about John. John was called the witness testifying to the light of God. Jesus is the true light of God and is able to give light to every man. Just as physical light is necessary for our life to exist, we need the spiritual light of God to fully exist. The light of the word of God in the Bible. This is God, Jesus and the Holy Spirit, and now we wait for the coming of the light of Jesus, to be born and come into our life and the world at Christmas. The light of Jesus shone in the world during His life and time on earth, and has been passed on through Christian disciples since He ascended into heaven. His light is available now to all who believe Jesus is the Messiah and Son of God. When Jesus came into the world all the dark spirits were afraid as they knew they could not stand in His light, and He banished many evil spirits during His ministry. We now know that with Jesus' final act of conquering death and being resurrected He broke the power of the Devil over man. We look forward to celebrating His birthday soon to be here, and we also look forward to His second coming when He will return to earth and His light will directly shine again over and through the whole world, and in heaven. We enjoy preparing for His coming birthday party. The decorations we have put up and the activities we have taken part in have all been done to praise God for this coming birthday. We look forward to feasting spiritually as much as physically and we like Mary want to praise God.

Further reading - Isaiah 61 v1-4.

Prayers - Lord, let the light of Your Son Jesus shine in the world and banish darkness and sin from the world.

Action -

Notes -

December 24 Christmas Eve

<u>John 17 v1 (NIV)</u>. *After Jesus said this, he looked towards heaven and prayed "Father the time has come glorify your son that your son may glorify you".*

This verse from John's gospel was at the time Jesus had come to Jerusalem at the Passover. A few days earlier Jesus had ridden, on a donkey colt, into Jerusalem with great celebration. Jesus prays just before He was betrayed and taken by the Jewish authorities and later to the Romans and soon after crucified. In this reading today we learn about Jesus asking God for help so that He can complete His ministry and fulfill God's will, that through His death and resurrection, salvation and eternal life become available to all people. He prays publicly, identifying himself clearly as the Son of God and more or less saying this was the right time for Him to fulfill His purpose. Jesus knew what was to come, that He was to be the chosen sacrifice to die for the sake of man's sins. As we know the rest of the Christian story we know that this was fulfilled by the later death of Jesus on the cross and His glorious resurrection and Ascension to heaven. This reading has again moved on from the Advent story, but it shows what was to come for the adult Jesus. He had prepared for this during His extraordinary life and was ready to fulfill His ministry and mission in this way.

At this time we must think if we are ready for the birth of Jesus. Jesus prayed to God and we need to learn how important that is and pray ourselves. Have we had time to pray and prepare spiritually? Have we attended to our secular preparations (have we done our shopping, cooking, entertaining, organizing, decorating, present wrapping)? Are we feeling fresh and ready, or tired and ready or possibly tired and not ready?

How amazing that God has made Himself known to us and comes to us as a human baby, prepared to fully experience and share His humanity and His divinity with all. God did not come to mankind in person but instead sent a special part of Himself so that we can understand Him more fully as the Father of creation. He elected to send His Son to earth as a baby and to grow to an adult and experience a truly human existence whilst being truly divine and holy. The baby was to be called Emmanuel which means God with us. This is the most special birth ever (and all other births are special also). Mary and Joseph were at the end of the long journey, both of the pregnancy and getting to Bethlehem from Nazareth, and expecting the birth any time. This was to be the end of man's long journey with God while waiting for the promised Messiah. We must praise God for this wonderful birthday to come. We hope we are not too tired to praise God and we must pray for God's strength for us now and for the future so that we can go forward and grow with God. Our time of Advent preparation and journey is now drawing to a close but we must get ready to journey on with our own Christian life, toward our own salvation and eternal life with God, Jesus and the Holy Spirit. Mary and Joseph knew they were about to meet Jesus and as Advent draws to a close we need to be ready to meet Jesus too. They had fulfilled their role so far, as obedient children of God, doing God's will and were now preparing to fulfill their new role for God as parents to Jesus.

Today then is the last day of Advent and we should thank God for giving us this time to deepen our faith in and our relationship with Him. We know now that Mary and Joseph proved to be good parents to Jesus, and we will continue to see this in the time after Advent. Then we will also see that God continued also to be a good Father to Jesus, and remains so to this day and will be eternally. We hope we have learnt to obey God and to do His will in our personal lives through this Advent time. We now look forward to studying the rest of the Christian story and trust we will remain obedient to God.
Therefore each and every year, the Advent story gives us new hope, as we remember the start of the Christian story anew and we prepare to remember and relive the entire Christian story in the Christian year to come.

Further reading - Isaiah 40 v28-31.

Prayer - Lord God, we thank You for Your promise and covenant with us of sending us Your Son Jesus, our Messiah and Saviour. We look forward with joy to receiving Jesus and pray we are ready now to receive Him. Thereafter, we pray we can come to love Jesus and try to become like Him ourselves.

Action -

Notes -

25 December   **CHRISTMAS DAY**   **Season of Christmas**

<u>Luke 2 v6 (NIV).</u> *While they were there the time came for the baby to be born and she gave birth to her first born, a son. She wrapped him in cloths and placed him in a manger because there was no room for them in the inn.*

A<u>llelujah, Christ is born. Praise God.</u> The baby Jesus is born and the family (father, mother and baby) are safe. All sorts of emotions are now released, primarily joy at this wondrous event. It must have been a difficult time for Mary and Joseph as there were no rooms available for them in a crowded Bethlehem. They had to accept refuge and shelter in a stable and provide a manger for baby Jesus, which was His cot (bed). They must though have been overjoyed at the safe arrival of baby Jesus, in fulfillment of God's promise to them. This is a very humble beginning for the Son of God, but again the family have accepted and trusted this as being the will of God. The Christian story has many paradoxes and this is another one as Jesus is seemingly an ordinary baby but in reality is an extraordinary baby born in an unusual place in circumstances chosen by God. Although He was fully human and dependent, He was also the divine Son of God. Throughout His life He had a close and special relationship with God. Nonetheless Jesus had many temptations to resist during His life, however He resisted them all and led a sin free life. Jesus the promised Messiah is born today and now all the Old Testament predictions about His origins have been fulfilled. God's plan now continues; for us to be able to reach Him via the crib of Christ, and then cross of Christ to come.

Furthermore this special birth was announced in a special way by the angels who told local shepherds of the event. The shepherds represented the common people. They were not civic officials, church leaders, or rich aristocrats, but they were responsible hard working people. Jesus Himself was later referred to as the good shepherd and He used shepherds Himself as examples of how a leader should look after his followers, and indeed He compared His role to that of a shepherd. They reacted to their angelic encounter and went to Bethlehem to see and honour the baby Jesus and to praise God for this miracle. When they had seen baby Jesus and done these things they left the stable and went to spread the word of all these events to all they met. The angels celebrate and praise God in heaven also. So the king of mankind is born in a stable in Bethlehem. Where is His kingdom? The answer is all around and anywhere in the world and also heaven, though especially in men's' hearts and souls. Just as His earthly kingdom was hard to directly visualise, so was His heavenly kingdom, of which He is the heir, and which remains for eternity. We have considered these matters during the days of Advent and now we focus on the birth of and meeting Jesus.

Today we can and should go to Church to meet Christ as the baby Jesus and we can bring presents for the new baby Jesus, what would we bring? Perhaps toys, food, clothing, money and valuables, and time and love. Now we give friends and family gifts, to show our love for one another and we can give to others we do not know personally, possibly to strangers, possibly to charities. We give especially to the Church and charity as our thanks to God for His gift of Jesus to us. Perhaps most of all we would try to give our love and to establish a relationship with the new baby. We need to give Jesus our lives, that we serve Him, as He came to serve us. We praise God for giving us His Son, promised Messiah. We thank God for His blessing of Jesus in Church and then we must do as the shepherds did long ago and go out and tell people of this marvellous event and birth of Jesus. He comes as a brother, and as a son, to us all, as all people are part of God's worldwide family. Jesus is God's present to mankind, and we thank God for this and rejoice (our Christmas present from God). Some of our gifts that we have given or received today may be expensive, but none are as special of this gift God has given us, which is truly priceless. To love Jesus and accept Him as our Saviour is a priceless gift, but it is a free gracious gift from God to us. To follow Jesus and love Him can be hard, as we must try and leave our sinful nature which can be difficult, but to do so leads to a fully joyous complete eternal life, thereby allowing everyone of us to fulfil our potential and to be with God. Simply there is nothing better than this. The only cost of Christmas was that paid for by God at Good Friday until Easter Sunday (when Jesus was unfairly crucified and died). There was rejoicing in heaven at Christmas, but pain and sorrow when God paid a high price at Good Friday, when Jesus died to take away the sin of man, but then rejoicing when He broke the power of death, and was resurrected three days later at Easter.

Today though is a very special day, a holy day, and holiday, to honour God. Many churches have held special midnight services, to greet the birth of Jesus, the Messiah at the very start of this day. These are often popular and many attend other services through the day. However for proper obedience to God it is best to go to regular Sunday church services and not only attend on high days and holidays (Jesus and Church is for life, not just for Christmas). In church, the central candle of the advent ring is lit, representing the light of God in the world as Christ. As we have seen through our Advent readings Jesus has constantly been present but unseen throughout Advent. Now on Christmas Day Jesus is revealed and seen and should truly be at the centre of our lives, as He now is the central figure in the nativity scene. <u>HAPPY BIRTHDAY JESUS!</u>

We don't know the details of the birth, whether help was at hand or not, or if it was difficult or not. We do know it did not happen in the ideal place, a stable or cattle shed after a long tiring journey and Mary and Joseph were probably tired. Although whatever pain and suffering the birth experience gave, the safe birth resulted in tremendous joy. Any birth is a special event signifying the start of new life, a blessing from God, and this was an extraordinary birth event. This joy probably gave fresh hope and strength to Mary and Joseph, but they will have needed rest when this dissipated.
Advent is now over and Jesus our Messiah and saviour is born and is with us. We should rejoice now and accept Jesus into our lives. Advent can be thought of as preparing for the coming of Jesus. Christmas can be thought of as the receiving of and sharing of Jesus.

Many people give and open presents and this especially excites children. Christians do this believing them to be similar to and representing the presents baby Jesus received. Others believe or pretend the presents come from Santa and participate in a different non-Christian, Christmas day event. Jesus is not, nor like, Santa, who only helps make toys and distributes them on Christmas Eve to be opened on Christmas Day. There is no place in the Christian Advent or Christmas stories for Santa. Jesus helps all people in all areas of life all the time, and so today the Christian Christmas celebration is solely about Jesus' birthday. Christians celebrate by thanking, praising and honouring God for the birth of Jesus, His Son, our saviour, and then need to share Jesus, and our celebrations, with any non Christians we meet. We often give presents to those we like and love, and in the same way, Jesus is God's present to all mankind whom He loves. Christians ought to give love and presents also to those people they do not like, following God's example of giving love to all people.

We Christians can celebrate now, and often we eat a special Christmas dinner, possibly enjoying more food and drink than usual. We may have party hats, sometimes from crackers, and play games, or just try and relax. While it is acceptable to feast we should not overindulge ourselves, to feel sick or tired. Hopefully we should not be full of alcoholic spirit but instead be full of the Holy Spirit. We should try to be generous and helpful and loving especially to those who have been organising the celebrations with cooking, clearing up, entertaining, probably making them tired. In England the Queen gives a public address to the nation. As head of the Church of England, she often encourages the nation to follow a Christian life. Many people though have no presents to give or receive, and no special Christmas treats to celebrate with, and we as Christians should pray that they too can be aware of God's Son entering the world today and that Jesus can enter into their lives as well as our own. We need to try to share our Christmas blessings with those that have few or no such blessings. Also normal life continues, and accidents and illnesses and problems unfortunately can and do happen. This means while some new babies are also born, other people may die. Some of these events today will bring happiness, while some will bring pain and unhappiness. We need to bring all our joys and sorrows to Jesus today, confident that He is here now and will help us and with time He will restore us to God, for our God given purpose.

Are we ready for Jesus now? Do we now care for baby Jesus? Hopefully we are ready, and we can enjoy being with and celebrating with Jesus now. We have had the Advent period to prepare, and if we have not prepared suitably, we are missing out now. The good news though is, Jesus the Messiah will take us just as we are, if we commit ourselves to Him. There are no exams to be taken and passed or any other requirements; all He requires is our will to love Him as God's Son. We also can and should love Him as our own son and by acknowledging that He is in fact the Son of God we will be able to receive His total love. If we can do that then we ourselves become born again in a spiritual sense. The Christian story continues however with the further time and events of the season of Christmas and the Epiphany to come.

Further reading - John 1 v14.

Prayer - Lord God, we thank You for Your priceless gift of the birth today of Jesus. You love us so much that You came to us in this special way, so that we may make our lives complete by coming to You through Your Son. Praise be to God, Jesus and the Holy Spirit now and forever.

Action -

Notes -

26 December - (Boxing Day) St Stephens Day
Season of Christmas

<u>Acts 7 v54-55 (NIV).</u> *When they heard this, they were furious and gnashed their teeth at him. But Stephen, full of the Holy Spirit, looked up to heaven and saw the glory of God and Jesus standing at the right hand of God.*

Today's reading and theme is of the stoning of Stephen. Briefly we leave the Nativity scene and have moved on some years in time, to a point after Jesus's life finished. Here we see how powerfully Jesus's life influenced those who believed in Him. Stephen had been filled with the Holy Spirit and was actively teaching about Jesus but was being accused of blasphemy. This led to him being stoned to death for his unshakeable belief in Jesus the Messiah. Stephen had been chosen by the Apostles as a helper to the early Christian Church and was given the title Deacon. Stephen was full of enthusiasm for Jesus, and he clearly accused the Jewish authorities of killing Jesus and not obeying God. They lashed out at him in this violent way, and yet he called out to God to forgive them. Stephen followed the example of Jesus who had also called this out to God to forgive those who crucified Him.

At this time a period of persecution started for the new Christian Church and part of this was led by a Jew named Saul who was later converted to a Christian and became known as Paul the apostle. This Jew, Saul was present at the stoning of Stephen and approved of this act. We have to realise that our belief in Jesus can lead to hardship (mainly from non-believers). It is part of our Christian duty however to state that we believe in Jesus to others, not only to fellow Christians but also to non-believers alike. The later conversion of Saul to the apostle Paul was an amazing event. It is a dramatic example of how when a person is close to God incredible events, even miracles, are possible. This can be an inspiration to us all. It means that no matter what our past has been (even if full of prior sin), we can be used by God, as long as we change and truly repent and accept Jesus as our saviour. Stephen is a well known Christian martyr and there have been many others through the years since, some known of, but many not known of. His death did not make things easier for anyone, people who are prepared to die for their beliefs are specially committed.

God though has only ever planned one person to die for others and that was His Son, the Messiah Jesus. God does not want anyone else to die unjustly, especially not meaninglessly, and without this action saving the lives of others. It is though possible to admire the strength of faith shown by such an act, and so be personally changed and strengthened. Stephen followed Jesus exactly, sharing a similar unjust death, and though this is extreme, it is not asked for by God or generally required by God. However, Stephen's death may well have been a factor in Saul's conversion to a Christian. Saul witnessed Stephens's courage and commitment to Jesus. This may be another example of how good can arise from evil things in unexpected ways. It is often said that God works in mysterious ways. Stephen's act has prevented Saul from going on and persecuting more Christians. Saul became changed into Paul, and as Paul, went on to help establish the early Christian Church and he suffered persecution himself for this. In fact he also was eventually killed by the Romans for his belief in Jesus as the Messiah and Son of God. Everyone is changed in some way by encountering Jesus, and God ensures this will ultimately be for good.

Today is another national holiday in UK. It can give us a moment to rest and reflect. We thank God for the past, the present and the future, and that He is with us always. He is God eternal. We believe He knows and loves us, fully confirmed by the arrival of Jesus. We can thank God for the way He chose to bring us back to Him through the life and then the death and resurrection of His Son, promised Messiah. We thank God for being with us and bringing us through Advent to Christmas and now to journey on. We also believe Jesus will come again and we can look forward to that time when we can meet Him ourselves in God's heavenly kingdom. It would probably have been a time when Mary, Joseph and Jesus were trying to rest and reflecting on what this time meant for them, while probably thinking of how life would be now and what God's plan was. They may not have been able to get much rest, as they were getting to know the baby, and trying to settle into a pattern (feeding, cleaning, eating, nursing, sleeping). Some babies have the ability to require lots of attention and at inconvenient hours. Others are described as little angels, who seem to require little attention and seem so sweet and well natured. Again it is conjecture how Jesus was as a baby, but I like to think that He was no great trouble and sweet and well loved and good-natured. Probably too sentimental a view!

Although today is a holiday, some shops open and sales begin. Indeed this is the time some people buy discounted Christmas cards ready for next Christmas. Eggstrodinarily(!) advertising for Easter egg confectionery has started, showing that the commercial world is already moving on to the next business opportunity.

Today was traditionally a day when poor people received money from churches. The money that had collected in boxes (also called alms boxes) was distributed (giving today the Boxing Day name). This was a custom started in the medieval ages, and it still continues today (alms to the poor, from the alms boxes).

Now we continue on our journey, in the season of Christmas. Advent was the very start of the Christian story and this story now continues and cycles through the remainder of this secular year and then on through the secular New Year to come.

Further reading - Acts 6 v5.

Prayer - Lord God, we pray for wisdom and strength for those in authority and that they are guided by You in all their actions.

Action -

Notes -

27 December - St John's Day
Season of Christmas

<u>1 John 5 v1 (NIV).</u> *Everyone who believes that Jesus is the Christ is born of God, and everyone who loves the father loves his child as well.*

The Church calls today St John's Day. John was one of Jesus' disciples and John's Gospel is a marvellous witness to God, and we have previously read from this. The reading today is from his epistle, a letter to the church to strengthen and help the churches' understanding and application of Christianity. John is known as an evangelist. We have seen earlier that John the Baptist is also known as an evangelist. All Christians are called to be evangelists, to proclaim the gospel, and to point people to God. We should encourage all to read the Gospels for an account of Jesus and to read all the Bible, Old and New Testaments, to learn about God, Jesus and the Holy Spirit.

Here John states that if a person believes that Jesus is the Messiah (the anointed one of God) it means they are born of God. Furthermore, if you love God the Father, you love Jesus the Son, and everyone else born of and so also, children of God. All Christians then are children of God and will remain so eternally. God is the parent of all people, and everyone who believes in God, Jesus and the Holy Spirit are His eternal children. This is a wonderful fact. Most, (though not all), parents love their children, and here we contemplate the fact that God loves all people and especially His children, meaning all those who love Him. Everyone can be thought of as a child of God. Christians believe everyone has been created by God and that God loves everyone. Not everyone though loves God, but those that do, acknowledge God to be their Father and they to be His children. All who believe themselves to be God's children believe they are figuratively and spiritually born of Him. By belief in God, Jesus and the Holy Spirit they believe they will have the eternal life God has promised to all His children. Some people believe in God, but do not believe in Jesus or the Holy Spirit. This may be through ignorance of the existence of Jesus and the Holy Spirit, but this does not mean they are denying God nor that God denies them. However if unbelief in Jesus and the Holy Spirit is by denial, then this implies denial of God and so also denial by God. John in this letter, reminds the Church that God is a loving God and that God calls all people to love Him and one another.

This then is what being a Christian is, a person who believes that Jesus Christ is the Son of God. The Christian church is composed of people who believe this. It takes a leap of faith to believe this, just as it takes a leap of faith to believe in God and also the Holy Spirit. No one can ever prove in human terms that God, Jesus and the Holy Spirit exist, and conversely no one can prove in human terms they do not exist. Christians believe there is overwhelming evidence that they do exist and so they have faith to believe in God, Jesus and the Holy Spirit. Christians believe God has created man and loves him and has given him freewill, to choose to have faith in God or not to have faith. God loves all men and has given us the choice, to have faith in Him or not. To have this faith means our relationship with God can be complete and two way, with faith in Jesus bringing us eternally to God.

Now we can continue to think of Jesus and His parents getting to know one another, and starting to grow up together. We continue to celebrate this special birth of the Messiah over and through this Season of Christmas. We know that the whole family would trust in God. Joseph and Mary had just started their new lives together as a married couple and now they were starting as parents. They would be reflecting on the events of the birth and visit by the shepherds, and planning for their future. They knew they were part of this extraordinary plan of God, but they did not know the full story of their lives or the life of Jesus their specially adopted son. They were living in faith daily, encouraging and supporting one another, and probably marvelling at baby Jesus. We know now, that they fulfilled their roles and looked after Jesus as if He was really their own child. All parents have a lot to learn about bringing babies and children up, drawing on their own experiences and with advice from others, and often learning at the time, from what works and what does not. Joseph and Mary will have been guided by their own Jewish upbringing and will have prayed for guidance on this from God. We now know they stand as good role models of parents for all to follow, and in the same way we can think of God being our Father, a point which Jesus emphasised in His ministry. God cared and provided for His special family then, and in the same way He cares and provides for His whole earthly family now, which we are all members of.

Further reading - Psalm 1.
Prayer - Lord, we thank You that You love us and sent us Your Son, both as our shepherd, and our lamb. We pray that we and all people can come to know Jesus and that everyone may love and praise You, Jesus and the Holy Spirit.

Action -
Notes -

28 December
Season of Christmas

<u>Matthew 2 v16 (NIV)</u>. *When Herod realised that he had been outwitted by the Magi, he was furious, and he gave orders to kill all the boys in Bethlehem and its vicinity who were two years old and under, in accordance with the time he had learned from the Magi.*

Today's Church theme is of the Holy Innocents, and we read about this today here in Matthew's gospel. The Nativity story continues with the Wise Men on their journey searching for the new King of the Jews. They came to Jerusalem and spoke with the current King of the Jews at the time, King Herod (Herod the Great). They probably assumed the current Jewish authorities would have been aware of the birth of a new Jewish king and would help them find the baby. The Wise Men, it is thought knew this event was due from prophecy within the book of Daniel from the Old Testament. This book of Daniel is full of prophecy, but the time the Messiah was expected was given in Daniel 9 v25-26. They were thought to have also seen a special new star, which was also prophesied as being associated with this event. The prophecy concerning the star is from Balaam, from the book of Numbers 24 v17, in the Old Testament. The Jewish authorities though seemed unaware of when the birth of the Messiah actually would be. Several other people had claimed to be the Messiah, but none had amounted to much and none achieved anything close to the national impact the Messiah was predicted to make happen. With these foreign dignitaries or princes arrival on a mission to find the Messiah, this would have affected Herod and he consulted his religious experts to see if they knew any more about this, and at least where the Messiah was predicted to be born. They told him it would be in Bethlehem, from the prophecies from Micah.

Herod was afraid that this new king might be a threat to his own kingship and authority. However he agreed to let the Wise Men continue their journey and search for the new king, if they would go back to him when they found him, and tell him exactly where the Messiah was. Herod said this on the pretext that he would then go and pay his own respects, when in fact he was probably planning to kill the baby. The Wise Men then duly continued on their journey and found baby Jesus in Bethlehem having been guided there by the star. They brought their gifts and honour to Jesus. It was not known exactly when the Wise Men found Jesus in Bethlehem, and although they are often placed in the stable and manger nativity scene, it is recorded they came to Jesus at a house. So they may have arrived just after the birth or they could have arrived a considerable while after the birth. The exact time of their arrival is not clearly recorded or known. It is known they had not arrived at the exact time of the birth and so placing their figures in the nativity scene on Christmas Day is not strictly accurate. Their importance in the nativity story is seen by the festival of Epiphany which celebrates their coming to Jesus and which we will soon be experiencing and exploring, as it follows the season of Christmas. Meanwhile, now returning to their arrival in Bethlehem to see Jesus, Mary and Joseph may have already taken Jesus back to Nazareth with them, and so may have left Bethlehem soon after the birth. They may then have returned around the Passover time and stayed there as they went to Jerusalem, and the Wise Men may thus have seen Jesus when He was a two year old and not a newborn infant. Whenever it was that the Wise Men exactly saw Jesus it was an important event (as we shall discuss more at Epiphany). Then, very importantly also, after they had seen Jesus, the Wise Men were warned in a dream not to go back to Herod and so when they left Jesus, they went straight back to their own country (Matt 2v12). When Herod realised the Magi had not done as he had asked them,(to return to him and tell him where Jesus was exactly), but had gone straight back to their own country, he was furious and gave an order to kill all the boys in Bethlehem who were two years old and under. Herod was not sure when the Messiah was born but made this calculation that it may even have been within the last two years.

The gospel accounts give two accounts from here. Matthew (Mat 2 v13) says then an angel appeared to Joseph, warning him to escape from Herod the Great and to go to Egypt with baby Jesus and Mary. The angel told Joseph that Herod was going to search for the child and intended to kill him. Joseph obeyed the angel and took Mary and Jesus to Egypt. Matthew continues saying this fulfilled the prophet Jeremiah's teachings "A voice is heard in Ramah with weeping and great mourning. Rachel weeping for her children and refusing to be comforted because they are no more". Critics say that this prophecy wasn't spoken about Jesus, but related to the despair felt when the Jews were taken into exile, by the Assyrians. As mentioned earlier, belief in prophecy can only occur if God reveals the prophecy to all conclusively, which Christians believed Jesus did in explaining scripture on many occasions. Fulfilment of prophecy is a powerful witness to God, but interpretation of this can be difficult and needs care, as wisdom, knowledge and judgement, are qualities necessary to be certain of the fulfilment of prophecy. Jesus had these qualities and we need to ask God, Jesus and the Holy Spirit if we have doubts about our own interpretation of scripture and fulfilment of prophecy.

Luke, (Luke 2 v39) then says Mary and Joseph and Jesus went back to Nazareth and does not mention them going via Egypt, but whatever route they took, they escaped the brutal killing of the baby boys and young boys in Bethlehem that Herod the Great committed. Herod had indeed felt threatened at the news of a new Messiah and as he now had lost his chance of finding who exactly this was, he responded by perpetrating this evil crime of having all these male babies and young children killed. This did not succeed as God helped protect Jesus, Joseph and Mary. This extremely cruel act of Herod's achieved nothing but misery (the act of a desperate and despotic person). This shows the consequences of sin can be appalling, and also points to the depths of unjust persecution that some waged against Jesus.

Matthew (Mat 2 v19-22) continues in his story that while Joseph, Mary and Jesus were in Egypt, an angel again appeared to Joseph and told him that Herod (the Great) had died and told him to return to Israel with the family. This was to persuade Joseph it was then safe to bring Jesus back to Israel. So Joseph obeyed this instruction, but he remained afraid of Herod's son Archelaus who now ruled in his father Herod's place in Judea, in Jerusalem. Herod Antipas (another son of Herod the Great) ruled the northern part of Palestine, actually Galilee and Peraea, that covered the area of Nazareth in Galilee. Joseph seemed less fearful of Herod Antipas, so decided to go and take the family back to Nazareth in Galilee and settle there, to keep a low profile and stay out of harms way. Archelaus in fact was only in power there for a few years before he was sent into exile by the Romans, because he had proved to be a bad ruler for his subjects and for Rome. Then a Roman governor was put in charge of the area in his place. The Roman Governor at the time of Jesus' ministry and later arrest by the Jews was Pontius Pilate, who finally ordered the crucifixion of Jesus. We have already mentioned that this fulfils the Old Testament prophecy, that the Messiah would be a Nazarene, which Matthew mentions here. Also this event of Jesus being called from Egypt was prophesied in Hosea 11 v1.

Today we can see how some have suffered a high price for Jesus God and the Holy Spirit. This ultimate high price has been paid for Jesus's safety. We should thank God for all those who have suffered and died in God's service and who will now be with God in heaven, because of this. We can also praise God that we personally have not been called to make this ultimate sacrifice ourselves and to pray and hope that if we were called to this, we would have the courage and faith to endure such a sacrifice for God.

Further reading - Hebrews 1 v1-4.

Prayer - Lord, we thank You for Your protection of baby Jesus. We pray You will keep us, and all people safe from those who mistakenly feel threatened by You and Your love.

Action -

Notes -

29 December
Season of Christmas

<u>Luke 2 v21 (NIV).</u> *On the eighth day, when it was time to circumcise him, he was named Jesus, the name the angel had given him before he had been conceived.*

Jesus is born in a Jewish family, and so according to Jewish law and custom is circumcised and named. This was done soon after birth and was not necessarily done in the Temple.
Here the baby Jesus is subjected to circumcision, which all Jewish males underwent. Circumcision was the physical act done to Abraham to remind him of the agreement (covenant) God made to him, to bless his descendants forever. It was then undertaken to all of Abraham's male descendants and so became an important Jewish tradition and act.

At this time also the baby was named, Jesus (Greek word) meaning Saviour. Now we call Him, Jesus Christ, and Christ (Greek word also) means Anointed (as does Messiah, the Hebrew word). Jesus Christ is Greek meaning Saviour Anointed. In Hebrew, Jehoshua Messiah. This was the name the angel Gabriel had told Mary to call the baby, and accordingly Mary and Joseph obey this divine instruction. The meaning of this name points to Jesus' mission to come as the anointed saviour for mankind. Jesus was brought up a Jew and experienced all the traditions and customs of the Jewish culture. This was significant, as the Jews were God's chosen people, and they were awaiting the saviour or Messiah that they believed God had promised to send them. Their devotion to God was meant to cover all areas of life, in the law, for daily living and of course for honouring God in religious practices. The Jews believed that many of these traditional customs and observances had been given to them by God, from the time of Abraham, then through their prophets (especially Moses) and leaders down the ages. The Jews had many customs to observe and often they worshipped God through these, and this gave the Jews their distinct national and religious culture and character.

As we have seen Jesus' birth fulfilled all of the Old Testament prophecies concerning the coming of the Messiah. Jesus was referred to as the new King of the Jews, and this was announced by the Magi who were seeking Him. Later in His life this expression was used to mock Jesus, for at His crucifixion the soldiers placed a crown of thorns on His head and a sign above the cross saying Jesus King of the Jews. Jesus may have been an unlikely candidate to be the new

Jewish king, as His father Joseph was a carpenter and not a rich Jew. Joseph though was descended from David who again had been Israel's most renowned king. David himself, as the youngest of Jesse's sons and a shepherd boy, again, had seemed an unlikely candidate for a king.

However we know Jesus came to earth to fulfill God's promised new covenant with all people and now no longer exclusively only the Jews. God had decided to honour all men equally again, possibly influenced by the Jews continually losing faith with Him, while many men from other nations were converted to worshipping God and often were more committed to God than the Jews themselves (e.g. Naaman see 2 Kings 5-on, and Matthew 8 v10). Jesus then came as a greater king than just the king of the Jews. He has come as the king of all mankind in heaven and earth and as the Son and Heir of the one high king of all in heaven and earth, God the Father. Jesus though came not as a king to be served, but He came to serve both God, and man.

The new covenant Jesus has brought has changed many customs (those to do with sacrifices and food for example). These outward signs have lost their importance, as what matters now are both inner and outer signs of people's love and faith in Jesus. Love of God the Father, the Son and the Holy Spirit matters more than symbolic cultural customs.

Further reading - Colossians 3 v16-17.

Prayer - Lord, let our thoughts and actions praise and serve You, now and always.

Action -

Notes -

30 December
Season of Christmas

Luke 2 v25- 32 (NIV). *Now there was a man in Jerusalem called Simeon, who was righteous and devout .He was waiting for the consolation of Israel and the Holy Spirit was upon him. It had been revealed to him by the Holy Spirit that he would not die before he had seen the Lord's Christ. Moved by the Spirit he went into the temple courts. When the parents brought in the child Jesus to do for him what the custom of the law required, Simeon took him in his arms and praised God, saying "Sovereign Lord as you have promised you now dismiss your servant in peace. For my eyes have seen your salvation, which you have prepared in the sight of all people, a light for revelation to the Gentiles and for glory to your people Israel".*

This is the time of purification of Mary as prescribed by Jewish law and custom, at the Temple, forty days after Jesus' birth. It was also the presentation of Jesus, as Mary and Joseph's son, to God at the Temple. At this presentation, Simeon met Jesus, and from that a tradition of celebrating with candlelight processions arose (because of Simeon's prophecy that Jesus was a light to enlighten the Gentiles).This has led to the day being called Candlemas and in many churches now candles are lit before the Holy Communion (Eucharist) service, but the celebration of Candlemas is not always held on this day, possibly because there are these other celebrations today. Mary and Joseph follow their Jewish culture and take part in this family event and dedication of their child to God. The family may have journeyed here from Nazareth or from Bethlehem, as the accounts are not clear what exactly happened to them after Jesus' birth.

According to the Law of Moses, a woman after childbirth had to stay at home and not touch anything consecrated to God, a state the Law called "unclean". Forty days after the birth of a boy (eighty after a girl) the mother was to bring offerings to the Temple, usually a lamb and a dove. The lamb as a burnt offering to honour God and give thanks for a safe birth, while the bird was a sin offering. For the poor, two doves would be acceptable instead of a lamb. Once this was done, the mother was cleansed of these legal impurities. We see that they sacrifice doves or pigeons as part of this event. This was the minimum sacrifice by Jewish custom and cost the least, showing that Mary and Joseph were not wealthy enough to offer a lamb.

The second ceremony observed by Mary and Joseph, was the presentation of their firstborn son Jesus. Again the Jewish custom was to offer the firstborn son to God and then ransom him back. Five shekels was the ransom paid by Joseph to the priest at the Temple. This ritual was to give praise to God for the birth of a first born son, as the firstborn son was deemed special and would be the heir of the family. This was a special time for the whole family, but this was made far more notable by the involvement of this man Simeon and his action of declaring Jesus to be the promised Messiah. We learn that Simeon was a faithful servant of God, who was prompted by God to go to the Temple at the time Mary and Joseph went with Jesus for the Purification and Presentation ceremonies.

Jesus' remarkable story continues with this pronouncement from Simeon. God did not let this time at the Temple pass uneventfully, but by this involvement of Simeon, pointed out the importance of Jesus. This would not have surprised Mary and Joseph, just further confirming Jesus' identity, and importance. It may well have surprised others, and may have surprised Simeon but he was very pleased as his life's ambition was now fulfilled. God by way of His Holy Spirit prompted Simeon to perceive who Jesus was. Simeon also predicted to Mary that Jesus would attract criticism and such things would cause her much sorrow. For Mary then this was a bitter sweet proclamation. She would have been pleased to hear that Jesus would serve God as the promised Messiah, though she would be sad to hear it would lead to so much sorrow of her own. Mary though seems to have such deep faith in God she seems to trust God at each and any stage of her life, and that she could deal with both joy and trouble with God's help. She accepted either if they were part of God's will and plan for her. Mary shows us that she was ready and prepared to make self-sacrifices to serve God. Then after this declaration from Simeon, a prophetess called Anna arrived and praised God for the child Jesus. This was a further testimony to the importance of Jesus.

Luke says little else about this except that the family leave for Nazareth. This is different to Matthew who says that the family fled to Egypt to avoid the wrath of Herod the Great who wanted to seize Jesus. Luke does not make an account of the Magi and Herod's role either. Whatever and wherever they went when they left the Temple, Mary and Joseph did everything they could to care for, look after and protect Jesus. They themselves do not appear to have disclosed or widely publicised who they believed their son Jesus was, namely that He was the Messiah. That was not God's plan for them as parents, instead they had to wait patiently and bring Jesus up normally and allow Jesus to fulfill His destiny. They were content to let others discern the importance of Jesus and for their own family future to be dictated by God's will. They would have been aware if they had widely publicised the Advent and Christmas story that they had just experienced, it would have caused a stir, which could even have endangered Jesus' life, and they had only had instruction from God to protect Jesus at that point. They had to trust further in God and be patient and await God's later instruction and guidance, for their new family life.

Further reading - Revelation 21 v1-4.

Prayer - Lord, we thank You that You fulfill Your promises to Your faithful servants and we thank and praise You for sending us baby Jesus, just as Simeon did.

Action -

Notes -

31 December
Season of Christmas

<u>Luke 2 v41 (NIV).</u> *Every year his parents went to Jerusalem for the feast of the Passover.*

Jesus had returned from Egypt with His parents back to Nazareth and was growing up there, and in today's reading we consider more events of his childhood, and are remembering Jesus' family life.

There is very little written in the Gospels about this time of Jesus' life. This is the account of the annual family pilgrimage to worship God at the important Jewish festival of Passover (the celebration of the start of the Jews flight from Egypt to the Promised Land, Israel). This must have been an important social and educational event for Jesus. Initially Jesus would have been guided by His parents and family and friends. However with each passing year He would be older and more mature. Up until Jesus was twelve years old it is assumed the trip had though been fairly routine. However as this passage continues it shows that this, His twelfth years trip, was different and exceptional. For when the festival finished, His parents, Mary and Joseph, went home as normal but Jesus did not go back and initially they were unaware of this. They travelled on for a day before they realised He wasn't with them and so they started to look for Him, and as they could not find Him they went back to Jerusalem to look. In all they found Him, three days later in the Temple courts sitting with the teachers listening and asking them questions. His parents were amazed as they were understandably anxious and they asked Him why He had done this and made them worried like that. His reply rather perplexed them as it was unexpected and they did not understand it. For Jesus told them He had been in His Father's house all the time and rather implied they should have known He was to be found there and that they had not needed to be worried.

Jesus was a Jew and studied the scriptures, but this passage implies He knew His true special identity as Son of God. We have earlier seen that Jesus had a great knowledge and understanding of scripture. Mary and Joseph knew Jesus' special origin from God of course, but they had other children and would not have treated Jesus differently to the first born male of any Jewish home. They had no riches or lands or kingdom. Jesus would have seen His father Joseph working as a carpenter and the family leading a regular normal working life. Here we see how important His other parenthood was to Him. Only Jesus the Son of God could say and it be literally true, that in the Temple He was in His Father's house. As we are all effectively sons and daughters of God's family we could say such a thing, but this would not be literally true as it was for Jesus. This passage shows how fully Mary and Joseph had come to think of Jesus as their own child, as evidenced when it was said they did not understand His reply to them of being in His Father's house. This was possibly the first major sign to Mary and Joseph, that Jesus was only their adopted son and was indeed the true Son of God, and it seems to have found them somewhat unaware and forgetful of this.

Today is the Christian western world's traditional New Year's eve, and tomorrow, as New Year's Day, will be the first day of the secular New Year (remember the Christian western Churches' New Year starts on Advent Sunday?). Now is a chance to reflect on the old year and plan for the New Year to come. The most important act is to remember that we have recently received Jesus Christ and we must let Him grow in and with us now and throughout this coming new year.

Further reading - John 15 v11-17.

Prayer - Lord, we thank you for the year that has past. Forgive us when we have not done Your will and lead us into and through the New Year, helping us to follow Your example and to try to be good like Your Son Jesus.

Action -

Notes -

1 January - New Years Day
Season of Christmas

<u>Luke 2 v51 (NIV).</u> *Then he went down to Nazareth with them and was obedient to them. But his mother treasured all these things in her heart. And Jesus grew in wisdom, and in favour with God and men.*

Here the reading concludes the story of the visit at Passover to the Temple that was started in yesterday's reading. It simply says that Jesus went back home to Nazareth with them and behaved well towards His parents especially. This follows the fifth Commandment given by God to Moses (honour your father and mother). Jesus though is again in a unique position in having, in effect, two sets of parents, His earthly ones and His heavenly Father God. However we also are sons and daughters of God in that He created us, but we were created human by God and not also heavenly like Jesus. Nonetheless we too have our earthly parents and God as our heavenly parent. Jesus was obedient to both sets of parents and we should follow this example and do likewise, being obedient to our parents and to God. Here we see the love that Mary had for Jesus. Some of the things Jesus did may have surprised her, but she had become and remained a loving mother to Him. She is seen in the Gospels in several more places and is notably present at Jesus' crucifixion. Joseph, however is not mentioned from this point on and some people think he died sometime after this and before Jesus started His ministry.

This passage, and somewhat briefly, really concludes the early life of Jesus. We see that Jesus was obedient to His parents (of course this fulfils the Old Testament commandment to honour your father and mother). Also as Jesus grew older He became wiser and He was well thought of by His divine Father and His own human family (especially his mother), friends and presumably acquaintances. Joseph and Mary had other children of their own, and Jesus had younger brothers and sisters, in that sense. Presumably, He will have experienced a relatively normal family life and upbringing. Joseph and Mary did not reveal to the neighbours or the world, Jesus' true identity, as they were not directed to do so by God. Instead they knew they had to keep a low profile to keep Jesus safe until God decided it was right for the next phase of Jesus' life to start. So they had to wait for the time God would declare it right for Jesus to make Himself known to the world. This upbringing will have given Jesus direct experience of human life, giving Him the understanding of physical and mental pain and pleasure. As a human, Jesus fitted in fully and would have come to understand human nature intimately, while being the perfect human.

All the while He was growing up, His body, mind and spirit were getting ready for His ministry (mission) to come. It is thought Jesus started His ministry when about thirty years old, and so He had a long period of possibly eighteen years still to wait, from this point, before starting His Messianic mission. This ministry then lasted approximately three years, during which He constantly called people to God, through belief in Him as the Messiah and Son of God.

From this time that we consider in the reading today, until the start of His ministry we have no more information from the Bible about Jesus' early life. This passage very briefly says Jesus was favoured by both God and men and became wise. So, Jesus grows up physically and mentally and spiritually and matures to the point and stage where He was ready to start His appointed ministry. We do of course know, that Jesus was waiting for the right time in Israel to start His work (ministry) and it was John the Baptist who started the return to God of the Israeli nation and who started to proclaim the coming of the Messiah. John's ministry acted as the catalyst to the start of Jesus' ministry, the events of which are detailed in the Gospels, and are explored in the Churches seasons in the year ahead.

Today, though, is New Years Day. It is a Bank Holiday in the UK and a time when people hope for a good New Year to come and people celebrate and remember the events of the last year. It is a time when people often make plans for the coming year and resolutions, often involving changing their lives, to better and make improvements to their and other people's lives. A good resolution for Christians and all is to do God's will and to be in right relationship with God. Once again Jesus has set us the example of this. It is a time for new beginnings and hopes for the world. This day does not coincide with the Christian Churches New Years Day, which is the first day of Advent. Nonetheless as a Christian each and every new day can be a day of new beginnings and fresh hope with God, Jesus and the Holy Spirit.

Further reading - John 14 v6.

Prayer - Lord God, we thank You for the past year, and we thank You for today. We pray for the future also, that we will be together with You every day of the New Year.

Action -

Notes -

2 January
Season of Christmas

<u>Matthew 17 v22-23 (NIV).</u> *When they came together in Galilee he said to them "The Son of Man is going to be betrayed into the hands of men. They will kill him and on the third day he will be raised to life". And the disciples were filled with grief.*

We have now moved even further forward in Jesus' life in this passage. Jesus has now begun His ministry and is speaking to His disciples about His future. God's plan for Jesus has been set and Jesus knows and understands this and shares it with His disciples. He tells them this well in advance to give them time to get prepared and to try to understand this course of events.

All the Advent and Christmas hope seems to have been dashed, with this statement. Jesus had many followers, though some followed Him still not knowing or believing that He was the promised Messiah. When Jesus predicts His own death He confirms the disciples worst fears, as they believe that His kingdom and rule will not happen if He is dead. The disciples were not certain He was the Son of God, divine and immortal. If they had been certain of this they may not (should not) have been so full of grief. Not everyone welcomed Jesus as the Messiah. Some people felt threatened and possibly confused by Jesus' teaching. Chief of these was Caiaphas, head priest of the Temple and president of the Sanhedrin, which was the Jewish head council. He could only see Jesus bringing radical change and this threatened the old and existing traditions and practises, and he felt his own lifestyle threatened by that. He also felt the way of life of the Jewish people, especially the ruling religious authorities, to be threatened by Jesus. The Messiah then had enemies, for a variety of reasons, but principally a lack of understanding and ignorance.

However the full significance of His foretold death would only become apparent to His disciples after the events had occurred. It is often said that hindsight is a good thing and often later we can look back at events with the benefit of more information and put the pieces back together to form the bigger picture, and it becomes clearer. Jesus again tells His disciples He will be killed, as we saw earlier (Matthew 17 v12). Here in today's reading, though Jesus goes further and also says He will be raised to life three days later. So gradually Jesus is telling them of God's plan for this part of His ministry. He knows it will be hard for them to believe and understand it. They were once again upset at this, for the reasons we mentioned before and they would need time to understand the claim that Jesus would be raised from the dead. They may have believed Him, as He Himself had raised others back to life from death, but they still would have many questions about this and their main reaction was understandably grief. Today we have the luxury of knowing the full story of Jesus and can study its meaning and significance more fully. In Jesus' story as Christians, we know triumph arose from potential disaster and this confirms our belief that with God even the seemingly worst situations can be made good. We are now looking for the final piece of the story which is to be the second coming of Jesus. This second coming of Jesus will be the last part of God's plan to establish heaven on earth and we cannot predict when exactly it will happen. We look forward to this and should prepare ourselves for it.

Further reading - Luke 21 v 25-28.

Prayer - Lord, we thank You for Your faithfulness and goodness. Thank You that Jesus came for all mankind and that by living and dying for us He triumphed over sin, so that we and all people can come and be with You eternally.

Action -

Notes -

3 January
Season of Christmas

<u>Matthew 18 v1-4 (NIV).</u> *At that time the disciples came to Jesus and asked who is the greatest in the kingdom of heaven? He called a little child and had him stood among them, and he said "I tell you the truth unless you change and become like little children, you will never enter the kingdom of heaven. Therefore whoever humbles himself like this child is the greatest in the kingdom of heaven".*

In today's reading we continue with Jesus' ministry and Jesus, here, is teaching His disciples about heaven and humility. The disciples are thinking of heaven in an earthly, secular manner, and are assuming a hierarchy exists there possibly based upon good deeds or praising God or on some other basis. Jesus though has once again to turn the disciples' view upside down and to refocus it for them. He tells them there is no structure according to adult and worldly perceptions in heaven instead but the only structure there, would be similar to one of the nature of, and one that little children would understand. The disciples were probably expecting a very different agenda for the Messiah and of the kingdom of Heaven. They may have expected Him to be similar to a king or other worldly leader and to take charge in a conventional worldly manner. God's plan however is very different as we now know. Jesus came as the servant king not to be served but rather to serve. Jesus is our example to follow, and we need to have that attitude of service to others and to God. Heaven is no place for selfish attitudes, and faults such as pride and vanity are not present. In heaven, man will not need recognition and reward as status from man, as there man will be fully aware of the recognition from God, and will be there to serve and please God. In this way in heaven, man and God will be complete and fulfilled. On earth now we must try to attain this state of relation between ourselves and God and we may experience moments of eternal heavenly fulfilment. When we die, we hope our souls will come to God in His eternal heavenly kingdom and experience true and eternal fulfilment.

At this time we are still celebrating the birth of Jesus. Though we have gone ahead to Jesus' ministry we can see that Jesus highlights the importance of children to God and the Holy Spirit. For Jesus childlike qualities of trust, innocence and humility were very important, and should be aspired to by adults, and Jesus confirms those qualities are important in God's eternal kingdom in heaven and on earth. Adults can lose these qualities, and can become hardened and cynical, which are not characteristics that please God or other people. Instead God instructs that the spirit of humility is worthy of a person and we recall Mary telling the angel that she would do God's will and praised God for choosing her as the mother to be of Jesus, as she felt herself to be God's humble servant. This quality of humility must not be over exaggerated, but needs to be a completely natural state, as children and others like Mary have. Jesus criticised those who pushed their pious religious practices, including fasting and prayer, to extremes, in order to try to impress men and not to honour God. Jesus pointed out that God knows the intention and will of every person and cannot be fooled by any of man's lying deception. Jesus through His ministry had a special relation with children and recognized they needed to be cared for well. He had been well cared for by Mary and Joseph as a child and seemed to have appreciated that. Jesus though cares for all people and had compassion especially for vulnerable people, often children and the elderly. Christians and all people should follow Jesus' example of loving and caring for children especially, but also all vulnerable people.

Further reading - 1 Peter 2 v1-4.

Prayer - Lord, we thank You for the gift of children, for their freely given love and we pray You will help us to try to follow their example, and remember that we and all people are Your children.

Action -

Notes -

4 January
Season of Christmas

<u>Matthew 18 v21-23 (NIV).</u> *Then Peter came to Jesus and asked Lord, how many times shall I forgive my brother when he sins against me? Up to seven times? Jesus answered "I tell you not seven times, but 77 times".*

Jesus is here again teaching His disciples how to live as a Christian. He teaches that forgiveness is a very important part of Christian living. To forgive, whether to your enemy or to your brother, can be very difficult but it is a central part of the new Gospel teaching. It can sometimes be just as difficult to forgive a friend who you may feel has betrayed or otherwise misused your friendship. Forgiveness follows from a spirit of love and generosity, and these are qualities that Jesus proclaims as essential for His followers to have. Here Jesus tells Peter that he needs to forgive many more times than he had imagined. In this manner we will be acting in a similar way that God forgives anyone who sincerely repents, even if they repeatedly sin. This again is hard to understand and bear if people keep sinning against you and you need great patience as well as great forgiveness, to bear this. Again this patient quality is one God encourages and we must be slow to get angry in these situations. Time is a great healer and we have seen through the Advent and Christmas Bible readings, several examples of sins committed which have eventually led to good things arising from these later. God, Jesus and the Holy Spirit are the best healers, yet in order to obtain their healing for ourselves and others, when we approach them we must not hold bitterness and resentment toward anyone.

Also forgiving one's brother may be hard but forgiving your enemy can be even harder, but it is something that Jesus says we have to do. We need to remember that our enemies are also our brothers and are also sons of God. We need to forgive them both, if they ask for forgiveness, or even if they do not ask for forgiveness. For many people this can be difficult and hard to do. God though will credit you if you can forgive, especially if forgiveness has not been asked for. God will also give the strength to forgive others. Love will conquer over any sin anyone commits. Love then brings forgiveness and restoration and God has shown us that He is the only perfect example of true love, as He has forgiven man's sin of killing His Son, in order to overcome sin forever so that we can come to God through His Son Jesus. Again we find that Jesus doesn't just say these things, He actually practises what He preaches. This is seen clearly through His trial and crucifixion several times, as Jesus repeatedly asks God to forgive those who are hurting Him. When we find it hard to forgive we must go to God, Jesus and the Holy Spirit, who will help us achieve lasting forgiveness. God forgives us when we have clearly wronged Him and we ask His forgiveness. God asks us to forgive those who have similarly wronged us whether or not they have asked our forgiveness. If they have not asked our forgiveness then we have to let God be the judge of them and us, and we can God ask to do this. When we ask God to judge anyone we must ask Him to judge us first and if we are at fault we are to do His will to put it right before God and those we have wronged. We may remember that all Christians and indeed all people have done some wrong in their lives. No-one is perfect, although Jesus is our example of a perfect life. If we are called to judge anyone we should first remember that. We recall what happened when Jesus told this to the crowd who wanted to punish the adulterous woman, and in the face of Jesus' comment no-one took the step of stoning her (John 8 v1-11). Only God can judge fully, fairly and impartially, and God is always ready and prepared to forgive. Forgiveness may or may not involve some punishment, depending on circumstances. It always involves a commitment to improve matters, to rebuild a relationship, and it is much better to take a positive constructive approach than to be negative and destructive which is what happens when we do not forgive.

Today we have looked ahead and considered this teaching from Jesus' ministry. If it has any direct relevance to our recent experience over Advent and now during the Season of Christmas, we must try to apply it. We remember that Jesus came to deal with our sin and we must be guided by His teaching about sin and forgiveness. We can now also apply this teaching throughout our whole lives in the future. Following Jesus involves a new approach to life, and some may feel this sort of commitment is beyond them. Jesus knows that all people are weak and will probably fail by their own efforts, but, with Jesus' help, people can be strengthened to try and be more able to achieve this new and more fulfilling way of life (see Ephesians 6 v18). Every time we fail, we can start again with Jesus and with perseverance we can succeed to be His faithful servants.

However now we continue to remember baby Jesus who is several days old, and think of Him as He grew up getting ready to undertake His ministry, which we reflect on and use to guide us today, and forever.

Further reading - Daniel 7 v9-14.

Prayer - Lord, we thank You for Your loving mercy and forgiveness to all who truly repent. We are truly sorry for our sins. We pray that we, and all people may know You and Your righteousness.

Action -

Notes -

5 January
Season of Christmas

1 John 3 v16- 18 (NIV). *This is how we know what love is: Jesus Christ laid down his life for us. And we ought to lay down our lives for our brothers. If anyone has material possessions and sees his brother in need but has no pity on him how can the love of God be in him? Dear children let us not love with words or tongue but with actions and in truth.*

Jesus ended His ministry by giving His life to save us from sin. This caused Mary His mother much pain and all His followers also. It certainly caused Jesus himself much pain and this caused God pain too. Jesus remained fully obedient to God and this perfect man endured an unjust trial and unjust death by crucifixion, causing Him extreme physical and mental and spiritual suffering. Jesus had enjoyed good times in His ministry. When He came into Jerusalem before the Passover and with the last Passover supper to come, He had lots of support from His friends and His large following. He enjoyed all His good times, and praised and thanked God for them. He always knew there was to be a hard final act for Him to complete and at the moment this came, His faith was severely tested by this. He knew He would take on man's sin and have to do this alone and separate from His Father, but He believed His Father's love would prevail over this extreme situation. He knew God would not take this situation away from Him, but that God would lead Him through it, and deal with it. God had told Jesus the plan (though how much God had told Jesus we can only speculate on) and Jesus believed His Father, in a similar way that Isaac had believed and been obedient to Abraham while Abraham was obedient to God. Jesus was sacrificed, however this fulfilled God's plan with Jesus breaking the power of death over man and He was then resurrected.

Jesus was proved correct, God had dealt with this situation and led Jesus through it. Jesus praised His Father for that. We too experience good times and bad times and need to be obedient to God through them, for God has a plan to use these for good, even if we cannot see or know His plan in the same way that Jesus knew God's will for Himself. If we stay with God we will ultimately find and understand the plan and reason why we experience good and bad. Thankfully no-one else ever has to face such a challenge as Jesus' mission. After rising from the dead, He remained on earth a short while in His resurrected state, no longer human, telling His disciples their instructions before He ascended to heaven. As humans we do sin in many ways, but as we have mentioned before, God will always forgive our sins if we honestly repent and ask His forgiveness. Jesus' dying for us on the cross is the bridge over sin by which we may now reach God eternally. Jesus' love for us was perfect and complete and He had to die to save us. Jesus the Messiah both lived and died for all men. John here is restating these facts and emphasises that we must not just speak or write of love but that we must show love with our actions. John calls us to live and die for our fellow men, our brothers. Jesus remains the ultimate perfect example. We are not called to die like Jesus, that was His destiny to conquer sin and no one can repeat that or needs to. That work is done, and we should live for God and try to die from our old sinful nature and be reborn in God, Jesus and the Holy Spirit. If we do this, when we meet God after we die, Jesus' life and sacrifice takes away our sins and we will be with God eternally.

John calls us to share everything we have with our brothers, in fact with all people. In fact he calls us to share our whole lives for others, in effect to follow the example of Jesus who came to serve both man and God, and not to be served. Jesus is a special king, a new type of king, the Servant King. We need to help other people if and when we see them in need, again just as Jesus did. There is a catch phrase, WWJD, which stands for What Would Jesus Do? Remembering and applying this to our lives, this reminder can help guide us, to do the right thing in all situations, which is what Jesus would do in every particular situation. So now that we are at the end of Jesus's Christmas story, we need to try to follow His teachings and so to bear fruit ourselves, which will eventually enable the kingdom of heaven to come to and reign here on earth forever.

This is the last day of the Church's season of Christmas and is the secular world's Twelfth Night of Christmas, and tomorrow will be the start of the celebration of Epiphany. In the other readings we see that Jesus, Mary and Joseph are back in Nazareth, back from Egypt. Today we will take down the Christmas decorations, and prepare to follow Jesus as He grows. We thank God for giving us this Christmas season with baby Jesus, for being with us and helping us celebrate over this time and we look forward to growing with Jesus, the Messiah our saviour, in our lives from now on.

Further reading - Matthew 5 v6.

Prayer - Lord, we thank You for all our Christmas celebrations, especially for all Your love and help to us at this time. We pray that now Jesus will guide us in all we do, especially in giving our help to others.

Action -

Notes -

6 January - EPIPHANY   The Season of Epiphany:
The manifestation of Christ to the Wise Men

<u>Matthew 2 v1-3 (NIV)</u>. *After Jesus was born in Bethlehem in Judea, during the time of Herod, Magi from the East came from Jerusalem and asked "Where is the one who has been born King of the Jews? We saw his star in the East and have come to worship him".*

In the Christian calendar the season of Christmas has ended now (and traditionally the Christmas decorations come down). Today is the start of Epiphany (meaning "appearance" and now celebrating the time the Wise Men met Jesus). The early Eastern Orthodox Church originally chose today, January 6, as Jesus' birthday while the Western Roman Catholic Church chose December 25 (which had been celebrated in Rome since at least as early as AD 336). When toward the end of the 4th century the Eastern and Western Churches adopted each other's festivals the modern 12-day Christmas season arose. In the secular world, today is known as the Twelfth Day of Christmas.

We have already discussed the Wise Men in the reading of the Holy Innocents in respect to their meeting Herod the Great, as they searched for the new king. Now we study them further, as they continued their journey to find the king the Jews called Messiah. These Magi are the men we now call the Wise Men. They came from the East and came searching for the new king of the Jews. They saw the sign of a new star in the sky, as the catalyst to start their journey. They believed this sign heralded the coming of the new king of the Jews who would be of world renown, and the star was to guide them on their pilgrimage to find this king. As already stated, they were likely to have been aware of the Book of Daniel, specifically Dan. 9 v25-26, which tells of the expected time the Messiah would be in Jerusalem (despite this reference highlighting Jesus' crucifixion and death). More significantly Balaam's prophecy (Num. 24 v17) tells that a star will arise to indicate the arrival of the Messiah, and they may have used that to confirm their association of the star and Messiah. There has been much debate about the nature of the star through the ages since this miracle occurred. Again, it is beyond the scope of this book to examine this any further, and as we have already seen, belief in fulfilment of prophecy and in miracles, is a matter for personal opinion. Christians and others do believe miracles are possible and are ways that God can interact with man.

Now when the Wise Men came to Israel on their quest, they went to Jerusalem, the capitol, and there they approached the current ruler of the Jews, King Herod the Great, to help them in their search. Herod didn't know much about this and seemed surprised but he became interested in their arrival and request. Herod consulted his advisers, who told them that it was prophesied that the Messiah would be born in Bethlehem (Micah 5 v2-5). Herod decided to leave them to find the Messiah and asked them to return to him and tell him where and who this Messiah was. Initially they agreed to do this, but after they had visited Jesus they had a dream in which God told them not to go back to Herod, so they changed their plan and went straight back home (Mat 2 v12). After they had left, an angel then appeared to Joseph and warned him to take Jesus and Mary and to flee to Egypt in order to escape Herod, who was to start searching for Jesus. Herod was very angry that the Magi did not return to him and he ordered the killing of the young baby boys. The Wise Men had initially put Jesus at risk when they first met Herod and he became interested in finding Jesus, but they and Joseph were obedient to God and their actions saved Jesus from death from Herod. It is interesting to remember that the Wise Men arrived in Bethlehem some time after Jesus' birth and so were not present at the nativity scene in the stable on Christmas Day. It is convenient now to put their figures with the crib nativity set: however as they arrived sometime after the birth it is recorded (Mat. 2 v11) that they came to Jesus at a house.

Not much is known of these men, so we have many questions about them. Many see them as representing the world come to seek Jesus and bring Him presents as offerings. The presents they brought were special though somewhat symbolic. Frankincense, for purification to enter to the presence of God. Myrrh, an embalming agent signifying death and the mortality of man, and Gold, for a king, and signifying worldly wealth. These were all somewhat ironic for Jesus, as He was not born as an earthly king, but Jesus came instead as the special representative of God the heavenly king. In fact Jesus had no need of any of the gifts. For Jesus was able to enter God's presence without purification by incense. He did not need an embalming agent as He Himself was immortal and later broke the power of death over mankind. He did not need earthly wealth, as being the heir to earth and heaven, all things were His, and so worldly wealth was not significant for Him. Also what became of the presents is not known and is open to speculation. The presents were somewhat incidental, and maybe more symbolic than practical. Instead what really was important was the visit and honour these men brought to acclaim Jesus, as the awaited Messiah, not just of the Jews but of all people. It is also not known exactly how many Wise Men there were. It is traditional to say there were three, and that each one gave a gift.

Some people say each of the Wise Men came from one of the three continents known of at the time of Christ's birth (Europe, Africa and Asia). They are not named either in the Bible, but scholars believe them to have been Caspar, Melchior and Balthazzar. They are thought to have royal heritage, possibly being kings or princes themselves. Several Old Testament writings are thought to be prophecies referring to them (see Is. 49v7 -Is. 60v3 -Ps. 72v10). They came from the East (possibly Babylon) and are remembered for the effort that they undertook in their search for Jesus. It was their wisdom and knowledge that led them to discern that a new Jewish king was to be born, and it was their wisdom that appreciated the need to seek this important person and to proclaim Him. It then took faith to come to search for Him.

These are qualities that we can see in them and hope God can bless us and all men with these same qualities. As foreigners they represent the first Gentiles (foreigners and non Jews) to come to Jesus, which is again given as evidence that Jesus came for all men, not just Jews. Their arrival in Israel must have caused a stir in high places and certainly will have been a way of publicly making known an important event had or was about to happen.

Jesus' birth is announced by a noticeable event in nature, the appearance of a new star, and this prompted these men partly to come to look for Jesus. It certainly pointed the way for them in their journey into the unknown. Apparently the star remained directly above Bethlehem and above the place where Jesus was. The star can also be thought of as an ultimate candle celebrating the birth of this very important person, baby Jesus.

What the Wise Men thought of the modest surroundings they found the new king in and the strange events associated with their journey is not known. However their mission was successful and after encountering Jesus they returned to their homes satisfied and changed and enriched by their epic experiences. Importantly they had been successful in their mission to find their king and the king they believed of all mankind and they were satisfied to have achieved this. Their journey was not finished though, as they had to continue to return home and then to tell everyone that they had been successful and that the king was born. While this part of their mission is only partly recorded in the Bible, there is evidence to show they did continue to acclaim the new king Jesus when they had returned home, in effect becoming the first Christians. With this achieved too, their mission and purpose was completed, and the start of the revelation of Jesus to the wider world had begun.

There are many stories about the Wise Men. One is that they had a special scroll written by Seth, son of Adam, which noted prophecies of the Messiah especially the star appearing at His birth. They watched for the star and prayed to be led to the Messiah through the generations until the star appeared. When they returned to their country they were said to have built a cathedral to worship at, and were said to have been baptised and later gave their possessions away to the poor. In the Christian Church they have become the patron saints of travellers and are often portrayed riding on their camels. For some Churches, Epiphany is a very big celebration, and in some countries (popular in the old Czechoslovakia, now split as the Czech republic and Slovakia) it is the representative Wise Men that bring presents to children on this day rather than being given presents on Christmas day.

What Mary and Joseph thought of these visitors is again not recorded, but it maybe thought that these special visitors further confirmed to them, the specialness of Jesus and of God and his plan for them and for mankind. From now on though, the life of Jesus illuminates the world and His light is the starlight men need to follow in their lives. This story of the Wise Men was the final part of the birth of Jesus, the Messiah and Son of God, and the whole event can now be seen as a truly remarkable and wondrous event.

Further reading - Isaiah 60 v1-6.

Prayer - Lord God, we thank You for the part the Wise Men played in the events of the birth and life of Jesus. Help us to be as faithful as they were and now journey on with You, Jesus and the Holy Spirit in our Christian life.

Action -

Notes -

Ending

This marks the end of this book, but in the Anglican Christian Church the season of Epiphany comprises of 4 Sundays.
The origins of Epiphany are from the Eastern Christian churches. Initially they included the birth of Jesus, the visit of the Magi, all of Jesus' childhood and up to His baptism by John. It was based around the Jewish Feast of Lights (Hanukkah) and as a fulfillment of this. However in Western Christian churches, Christmas was given prominence and fixed on 25 December, and so with the Eastern churches celebrating the Epiphany on 6 January, this has led to the twelve day season of Christmas (between the Advent and Epiphany seasons).

In the Anglican churches calendar, the season of Epiphany is then followed by:
The Presentation of Christ in the Temple (Candlemas).

For the sake of completion here, the Anglican yearly calendar continues as follows:
There are 5 Sundays before Lent.
The Season of Lent then begins on Ash Wednesday and then there are 5 Sundays of Lent.
This is followed with Palm Sunday.
Then there is Holy week - ending in Easter Sunday.
Then there are 6 Sundays of Easter, then Ascension day, then Pentecost.
Next is Trinity Sunday, and then there are 22 Sundays after Trinity.
Then there is All Saints day.
Then there are 4 Sundays before Advent and then Advent of the new year starts with Advent Sunday.

Appendices (extra food for thought)
Appendix 1
A brief comparison of the seasons of Advent and Lent

Advent is the time before Christmas, the birth of Jesus Christ.
Lent is the time before Easter, the death and resurrection of Jesus Christ.

As such, both are important Christian seasons in the Christian Churches yearly calendar.

Some Christians seem to promote and prefer one event (either Christmas or Easter) more than the other. It seems to me however that each event must have equal importance in the Christian story to date. Some Christians try to argue that the resurrection of Jesus is the most important point of the Christian story to date, and that as such Easter should be more prominent than Christmas. I however firmly feel that the birth and incarnation of Jesus at Christmas is of equal importance to the death and resurrection of Jesus at Easter. I feel both events are in fact mutually dependent i.e. one event could not happen without the other, and are integral parts of God's plan in sending His Son to man, as Messiah and Saviour. As Christians we need to celebrate both accordingly but this does not mean we may not have a personal preference for either the celebration times of Christmas or Easter.

Advent and Lent are periods of preparation before Christmas and Easter respectively.

Lent is often thought of as a time of giving things up, as a help to action and contemplation on spiritual matters. Lent represents Jesus' time in the wilderness where He was tempted by the Devil and prepared Himself for His coming ministry, and later the death and resurrection of Jesus at Easter.

Advent is often thought of the as the time of taking things up as a help to action and contemplation on spiritual matters, in preparation for the birth and incarnation of Jesus at Christmas.

Lent is associated as a period of fasting before the feast celebration at Easter. Advent is not associated with fasting and precedes the feast of Christmas. There are various traditional foods associated at these times. Shrove Tuesday, Pancake Day precedes Lent, and pancakes, Simmnel cake, Leven and unLeven breads are made and eaten before fasting through Lent. Lent is a time of trying to live basically, in order to be near to God, and to hunger for God. Then at Easter, a celebratory feast is enjoyed and other foods are made and eaten, notably chocolate eggs and hot cross buns.

Advent is a time to honour God in, with and for, all the rich blessings God provides us with, especially contemplating new God given life developing and leading to Jesus' birthday celebration. Advent foods may include mince pies and Christmas foods include Christmas puddings, cakes and turkey dinners.

Many Church traditions are remembered at Advent and Lent. Advent preparation for Christmas is by reaching out. Lent preparation for Easter is by reaching in.

Both Advent and Lent are times to focus in on God, Jesus and the Holy Spirit.

At the end of both Advent and Lent we are given a gift or present from God. At Christmas, it is the wonderful birth of Jesus, Son of God and Messiah. At Easter, it is the triumphant resurrection of Jesus, risen from the dead, later to ascend to heaven. Therefore at both Christmas and Easter we give one another gifts and we ought to give a gift to God. Christmas and Easter also share certain features, particularly those associated with birth and new life.

Many people, especially children, may understand Advent more readily as it is the time spent getting ready for a birth, in contrast to Lent, which in effect, is the time spent getting ready for a death. Advent may be more cheerful while Lent may be more sombre. Miracles from God happen during both these times, and Jesus Himself is a wonderful miracle, Son of God and Son of Man. The secular world promotes commercial activities during both Advent and Lent and Christmas and Easter. The secular world promotes father Christmas, or Santa Claus, and the mid winter solstice at Advent, and at Lent the secular world promotes the beginning of season of spring (chocolate eggs and bunny rabbits). The religious world promotes spiritual activity concentrating on Jesus at all these times, especially emphasising new beginnings with God and man.

Advent varies in length, but Christmas is a set day every year on 25th December. Whereas Lent is a period of 40 days but Easter Day is not a set day but varies according to calendar variations.

In the Northern Hemisphere, Advent and Christmas occur in midwinter, while in the Southern Hemisphere they occur in midsummer.
Similarly in the Northern Hemisphere Easter is around springtime whereas in the Southern Hemisphere it is around autumn time.

Appendix 2
Glossary

Advent	From the Latin, and meaning coming, it refers to the Church's Season before Christmas, the coming birth of Jesus
Angel	Heavenly messenger and helper of God
Annunciation	The proclamation to Mary of Jesus' birth by the Angel Gabriel
Apostle	Originally one of the 12 chosen and sent by Jesus to preach the gospel - later applied to prominent people who took this mission from Christ to man (notably St Paul called himself an Apostle)
Ascension	After His death, Jesus was resurrected and stayed on earth a while. He then went to heaven, His ascension
Bible	Holy book containing the word of God revealed to and written by inspired servants of God (various translations exist in various languages, early versions in Greek and Latin, from original Hebrew manuscripts. English versions now include New International Version, NIV; Revised Standard Version, RSV; Good News Bible, GNB; King James Version, KJV,)
Christ (Greek)	Anointed (In Hebrew-Messiah)
Christian	Person who believes Jesus Christ is the Son of God
Christmas	Two words together Christ (Anointed) and Mass (religious observance)-Holy day celebrating the birth of Jesus, God's Son
Covenant	Agreement, often between God and man
Devil	Disobedient fallen angel, banished by God out of heaven permanently. Responsible for encouraging man to commit sins and works of evil. Also called Satan (and known by many other names e.g. Beelzebub)
Disciple	Follower and believer of Jesus
Epiphany	Manifestation of Jesus to the Wise Men (i.e. Jesus' appearance in the world)
Evangelist	Writer and preacher of the Gospel

Gentile	Any person of non Jewish faith, a foreigner to Jews
Gospel	Life and teaching of Jesus Christ contained in 4 Books of the New Testament (Greek word, literally meaning Good news)
Hebrew	Descendent of Abraham and also the language of these people, often called Jews
Heaven	To be in the presence of God eternally. Eternal kingdom ruled by God
Hell	To be unable to be in the presence of God eternally. Eternal kingdom ruled by Satan
I/E-mmanuel	Latin word meaning, God is with us
Incarnation	God, as His Son, Jesus, being made flesh/human
Jesus (Greek)	Saviour (In Hebrew, Yehoshua- Yeshua ben Yosef, Jesus son of Joseph)
Jew	Person who believes in God and follows Jewish cultural faith observances. Originally from the tribe of Judah
Magi	Wise Men (from Persian, meaning magician)
Messiah	Anointed deliverer (In Hebrew – Mashiach; In Greek - Christ)
Ministry	Special work for God
Nativity	Birth of Jesus
Pagan	Person who has no religious beliefs
Resurrection	Raised from death to life
Repentance	Regret of wrongdoing
Religion	Faith in a particular spiritual belief, doctrine, or Creed
Satan	The Devil - Disobedient fallen angel, banished by God out of heaven permanently and a corrupting influence over man. Presides in, and over Hell.
Secular	Not spiritual, not sacred – Non religious, and of the world
Spiritual	Divine holy matters of the spirit and soul - not of the world

Appendix 3
Alphabetical list of Advent, Christmas and Epiphany activities

A	Acting, Adoring, Administrating, Asking, Assisting, Attending
B	Behaving, Building
C	Caring, Changing, Cleaning, Communicating, Cooking, Constructing, Counselling, Creating, Cultivating
D	Daring, Dancing, Decorating, Drinking, Disciplining, Dying
E	Eating, Encouraging, Evangelising, Employing, Entertaining, Enjoying, Enthusing, Educating
F	Fasting, Feeding, Feasting, Forgiving, Fulfilling
G	Giving, Greeting, Growing
H	Healing, Helping, Hearing, Hoping
I	Instructing, Inspiring
J	Juggling, Jumping, Judging
K	Kissing, Knowing, Kneeling
L	Loving, Learning, Listening, Living
M	Maintaining, Marvelling, Managing, Meaning, Meditating, Meeting, Mending, Moving
N	Numbering, Naming
O	Occupying, Organizing
P	Praising, Praying, Planning, Playing, Planting, Producing
Q	Querying
R	Reading, Receiving, Relaxing, Rejoicing, Resting, Respecting, Running
S	Serving, Sleeping, Singing, Sharing, Shopping, Socialising, Studying, Supporting
T	Thinking, Training, Travelling, Talking, Tolerating, Tiring, Timing
U	Understanding, Uplifting
V	Valuing
W	Waking, Walking, Working, Worshipping, Wanting, Writing
X	eXclaiming !
Y	Yawning
Z	Zephaniahing!

These are some of the adjectives used in this book (and some which aren't!) ending in ING, and listed in alphabetical order. They describe many activities and characteristics that can be encountered during these seasons. Of course there are many other possible ones to include also. Think of the Advent, Christmas and Epiphany interpretation and relevance of these, and add any others you can think of. Let us honour Jesus the Messiah and Son of God, who is God's gift of fulfilment, given to man at the end of Advent and through Christmas and Epiphany and beyond. So we place God, Jesus and the Holy Spirit at the centre of our lives now and forever.

Appendix 4
Advent, Christmas and Epiphany Planner/Calendar

SEASON	DAYS	PLANS
A D V E N T	Advent Sunday 1	
	Mon	
	Tues	
	Wed	
	Thu	
	Fri	
	Sat	
	Advent Sunday 2	
	Mon	
	Tues	
	Wed	
	Thu	
	Fri	
	Sat	
	Advent Sunday 3	
	Mon	
	Tues	
	Wed	
	Thu	
	Fri	
	Sat	
	Advent Sunday 4	
	Mon	
	Tues	
	Wed	
	Thu	
	Fri	
	Christmas Eve	
C H R I S T M A S	Christmas Day	
	Boxing Day	
	27 December	
	28 December	
	29 December	
	30 December	
	31 December	
	1 January	
	2 January	
	3 January	
	4 January	
	5 January	
EPIPHANY	6 January	

Appendix 5
Your own notes
Start of Advent, Christmas & Epiphany Seasons - Aims:

Finish of Advent, Christmas & Epiphany Seasons - Achievements/ Comments:

Appendix 6   Days Of Advent Table

Date	Year 1	Year 2	Year 3	Year 4	Year 5	Year 6	Year 7
November 27	Advent Sunday						
28	Advent 1 Day 2	Advent Sunday					
29	Advent 1 Day 3	Advent 1 Day 2	Advent Sunday				
30	Advent 1 Day 4	Advent 1 Day 3	Advent 1 Day 2	Advent Sunday			
December 1	Advent 1 Day 5	Advent 1 Day 4	Advent 1 Day 3	Advent 1 Day 2	Advent Sunday		
2	Advent 1 Day 6	Advent 1 Day 5	Advent 1 Day 4	Advent 1 Day 3	Advent 1 Day 2	Advent Sunday	
3	Advent 1 Day 7	Advent 1 Day 6	Advent 1 Day 5	Advent 1 Day 4	Advent 1 Day 3	Advent 1 Day 2	Advent Sunday
4	Advent 2	Advent 1 Day 7	Advent 1 Day 6	Advent 1 Day 5	Advent 1 Day 4	Advent 1 Day 3	Advent 1 Day 2
5	Advent 2 Day 2	Advent 2	Advent 1 Day 7	Advent 1 Day 6	Advent 1 Day 5	Advent 1 Day 4	Advent 1 Day 3
6	Advent 2 Day 3	Advent 2 Day 2	Advent 2	Advent 1 Day 7	Advent 1 Day 6	Advent 1 Day 5	Advent 1 Day 4
7	Advent 2 Day 4	Advent 2 Day 3	Advent 2 Day 2	Advent 2	Advent 1 Day 7	Advent 1 Day 6	Advent 1 Day 5
8	Advent 2 Day 5	Advent 2 Day 4	Advent 2 Day 3	Advent 2 Day 2	Advent 2	Advent 1 Day 7	Advent 1 Day 6
9	Advent 2 Day 6	Advent 2 Day 5	Advent 2 Day 4	Advent 2 Day 3	Advent 2 Day 2	Advent 2	Advent 1 Day 7
10	Advent 2 Day 7	Advent 2 Day 6	Advent 2 Day 5	Advent 2 Day 4	Advent 2 Day 3	Advent 2 Day 2	Advent 2
11	Advent 3	Advent 2 Day 7	Advent 2 Day 6	Advent 2 Day 5	Advent 2 Day 4	Advent 2 Day 3	Advent 2 Day 2
12	Advent 3 Day 2	Advent 3	Advent 2 Day 7	Advent 2 Day 6	Advent 2 Day 5	Advent 2 Day 4	Advent 2 Day 3
13	Advent 3 Day 3	Advent 3 Day 2	Advent 3	Advent 2 Day 7	Advent 2 Day 6	Advent 2 Day 5	Advent 2 Day 4
14	Advent 3 Day 4	Advent 3 Day 3	Advent 3 Day 2	Advent 3	Advent 2 Day 7	Advent 2 Day 6	Advent 2 Day 5
15	Advent 3 Day 5	Advent 3 Day 4	Advent 3 Day 3	Advent 3 Day 2	Advent 3	Advent 2 Day 7	Advent 2 Day 6
16	Advent 3 Day 6	Advent 3 Day 5	Advent 3 Day 4	Advent 3 Day 3	Advent 3 Day 2	Advent 3	Advent 2 Day 7
17	Advent 3 Day 7	Advent 3 Day 6	Advent 3 Day 5	Advent 3 Day 4	Advent 3 Day 3	Advent 3 Day 2	Advent 3
18	Advent 4	Advent 3 Day 7	Advent 3 Day 6	Advent 3 Day 5	Advent 3 Day 4	Advent 3 Day 3	Advent 3 Day 2
19	Advent 4 Day 2	Advent 4	Advent 3 Day 7	Advent 3 Day 6	Advent 3 Day 5	Advent 3 Day 4	Advent 3 Day 3
20	Advent 4 Day 3	Advent 4 Day 2	Advent 4	Advent 3 Day 7	Advent 3 Day 6	Advent 3 Day 5	Advent 3 Day 4
21	Advent 4 Day 4	Advent 4 Day 3	Advent 4 Day 2	Advent 4	Advent 3 Day 7	Advent 3 Day 6	Advent 3 Day 5
22	Advent 4 Day 5	Advent 4 Day 4	Advent 4 Day 3	Advent 4 Day 2	Advent 4	Advent 3 Day 7	Advent 3 Day 6
23	Advent 4 Day 6	Advent 4 Day 5	Advent 4 Day 4	Advent 4 Day 3	Advent 4 Day 2	Advent 4	Advent 3 Day 7
24	Christmas Eve	Christmas Eve	Christmas Eve	Christmas Eve	Christmas Eve	Christmas Eve	Christmas Eve
25	Christmas Day	Christmas Day	Christmas Day	Christmas Day	Christmas Day	Christmas Day	Christmas Day

Appendix 7
Miscellaneous resources

Essential Reading: *The Bible* - (any version, NIV, RSV, GNB, KJV etc)

Other Reading: *A Feast For Advent,* D Smith
-BRF, ISBN 0 900164 61 1

Advent Readings From Iona, Woodcock/Pickard
-Wild Goose Publications, ISBN 1-901-55733-2

The Christmas Mystery, Jostein Gaarder
-Orion Books, ISBN 1-84255-050-0

Other material: Internet Sites - www.whychristmas.com
- www.newadvent.org
- www.shalfleet.net/advent/index.htm

Music: CD WOW Christmas -EMI Christian Music Group
080688607821
CD Handel's Messiah -London Festival Orchestra,
Ross Pople, ArteNova Classics 7 43214 18492 9

Prayer.
Lord God - We thank You and praise You for the times of Advent, Christmas, and Epiphany, leading to the birth and presence of Your Son, our saviour. Let all we do during these times be to Your service and for Your praise and to glory and honour You, Your Son and Your Spirit. Allelujah, praise to You forever, Amen.